1989

Jess F. Row

$2.00
10-7-20

My life in 250 words or less:

I was born in 1957 on a farm in Tennessee. I stayed there till I was 18, shirking various tasks such as gardening and tending animals. I also went to school in Nashville, a.k.a. Music City, USA, a.k.a. The Athens of the South. There I learned how to play the banjo and juggle and things like that. In 1957 I went to Princeton, didn't like it much, went to Nashville and got a job in a warehouse, which made Princeton look better. So I went back. I decided to try to do a double major in English and Creative Writing. I wrote *The Structure and Meaning of the Telephone Company* in my senior year. When it was finished I took a job as a sound man for a documentary film about re-forming junkies, in New York. When the film was finished I went back to Princeton, took exams and graduated. By this time it was 1979. I moved to a Spanish slum in Hoboken and sat around waiting for something to happen, but nothing did for a long time. I spent a lot of time in Washington Square, where the admission is free. In the fall I moved to a Spanish slum in Brooklyn and ran out of money. I started working at The Franklin Library as a part-time clerk and somehow crossed over into being a free-lance writer for them. That work is still my principal legitimate employment. In 1980 I went to Hollins College, VA and began writing *The Story-telling Stone*; I got an MA from Hollins in 1981 and moved back to Brooklyn, where I finished the book.

One of the other things I do is be a director of 185 Corporation, an artists' cooperative which does all sorts of interesting stuff.

Every word of this is the truth.

Madison Smartt Bell

Also by Madison Smartt Bell in Abacus:

WAITING FOR THE END OF THE WORLD
STRAIGHT CUT
THE YEAR OF SILENCE

Zero
db

✦

AND
OTHER
STORIES

Madison
Smartt
Bell

SPHERE BOOKS LTD

Published by the Penguin Group
27 Wrights Lane, London w8 5tz, England
Viking Penguin Inc., 40 West 23rd Street, New York, New York 10010, USA
Penguin Books Australia Ltd, Ringwood, Victoria, Australia
Penguin Books Canada Ltd, 2801 John Street, Markham, Ontario l3r1b4
Penguin Books (NZ) Ltd, 182–190 Wairau Road, Auckland 10, New Zealand

Penguin Books Ltd, Registered Offices: Harmondsworth, Middlesex, England

First published in Great Britain by Chatto & Windus Ltd, 1987
Published in Abacus by Sphere Books Ltd, 1989
1 3 5 7 9 10 8 6 4 2

Copyright © Madison Smartt Bell 1987
All rights reserved

The following stories in this collection have previously appeared elsewhere: "Triptych I," *The Crescent Review*; "The Naked Lady," *The Crescent Review*: "Monkey Park," *The Hudson Review*; "Triptych II," *Best of Intro*; "The Structure and Meaning of Dormitory and Food Services," *Lowlands*; "Irene," *Columbia*; "The Lie Detector," *The Crescent Review*; "I♥NY," *Green Mountains Review*; "The Forgotten Bridge," *Witness*; "Zero db," *Harpers*.

Printed and bound in Great Britain by
Richard Clay Ltd, Bungay, Suffolk

Except in the United States of America,
this book is sold subject to the condition
that it shall not, by way of trade or otherwise,
be lent, re-sold, hired out, or otherwise circulated
without the publisher's prior consent in any form of
binding or cover other than that in which it is
published and without a similar condition
including this condition being imposed
on the subsequent purchaser

To Cork and Gwen and Jane and Deborah (as always),
to all my students at Goucher and the 92nd Street Y,
to Marty, to Mike Sheehan and James Steigenwald
and all the lads at Sheehan's, I take off
my hat on this occasion

For Beth

BEFORE COMPLETION

CONTENTS

I

II

III

I

Triptych I

✦

THE TREE LINE at the top of the ridge was stirred by wind so that the light snow fell off the branches and scattered down the ragged slope. The snow parted in grains before the wind and settled in the low places. Not enough had fallen to coat the long gully that ran down the hillside and the gully lay bare, a reddish slash in the pale skein of snow. No snow stuck to the old disk harrow or to the pump at the bottom of the gully and these dark forms were outlined sharply, like the dark trees against the sky. Their iron was so cold it would burn skin at the touch. The iron latch of the gate near the foot of the hill was cold too, so that no one wanted to put his bare hand to it. The wind swept down around the gray board house and carried the smoke from the chimney down to the ground. The men working in the yard all ducked their heads away from it. The wind blew across Lisa's face, disturbing her pale hair and bringing water into her eyes. In a moment it was calm again.

Lisa was well wrapped against any kind of cold, with her corduroy coat down to her knees and her jeans stuffed into red rubber boots. She sat cross-legged on top of a washtub by the table where some women were cleaning chitlins. The sharp smell didn't bother her; it was alien and exciting. She was five years old and without prejudice. Her hair and skin were white enough to make her an albino, but her eyes were ordinary gray. The hog killing animated her and she couldn't sit still for long.

Jack Lee and Luther were working over the hog in the long scalding trough. The steam from the water mingled with the smoke of the fire under it, and there was thin vapor coming from the mouths of the two men, who were holding the carcass half out of the water with a length of iron chain. They turned the hog over with the chain to scald it evenly and pulled large clumps of bristles off with their hands. Hair and patches of scum floated on the surface of the cloudy water. When the bristles began to come away easily they raised the hog out of the water and rolled its body onto a bare board platform that was against one side of the trough. Then they scraped and shaved the hair away with big knives, occasionally rinsing the skin with hot water.

The hog's eyes were clenched shut and his jaws were locked together. Lisa scratched a white line along his flank with a scraping disk. It amused her to see the hair coming off in the wide places, but when they had to work closely around the joints and the head the job became difficult and boring. Lisa set her scraper down on the platform and ran off to the shed where the women were trimming scraps for sausage.

Amelia Tyler and Elizabeth were chopping the meat under the shelter. Their black hands moved rapidly across the planks, slicing some of the fat away from the lean meat so the sausage wouldn't turn out too greasy. From time to time they wiped their hands on the fronts of their aprons, and the aprons were blotched brown. Amelia had on a thick coat with the stuffing coming out in places, and her hair was pulled back from her forehead under a bandanna. There was a dent in the front of her head that a small hen's egg could have fit into and she had once told Lisa that something bad had been growing in there and they had cut it out in the hospital. They had talked about it all one evening when Amelia was Lisa's baby sitter.

Amelia pushed some of the extra fat over to Lisa and gave her a knife to cut it with. Lisa sliced the strips of fat into small square chunks, and Amelia said for her to take it out and put it in the cracklin pot. There was a big iron kettle in a frame over a fire outside and Lisa dropped the little squares of fat into it to render and make the cracklins. Some of them were already done and she dipped one from the surface of the water. It was crisp and golden but it had very little taste at all, and she didn't really want to eat another one.

Over near the scalding trough there was a thick pole lashed to the forks of two trees and four of the seven hogs were hanging from it waiting to be cleaned. The hogs were suspended from pointed sticks which were thrust over the pole and through the tendons of their hind legs, so that the hogs hung head down. Their heads aimed blindly at the frozen ground, and the slashes in their throats were bloodless now and white. They had been scalded and scraped and their bare skin was blue and gray, the color of a bruise. All seven of them belonged to Mrs. Denmark, who was Lisa's mother, but two of them would go to Amelia and Ben Tyler to help pay for all the work they did. They would take the heads and chitlins of all seven hogs too, because white people didn't eat those things.

Ben Tyler was up on the road where the cars were, with Luther. They were sharing bootleg whiskey from a flat unmarked bottle. Looking up there, Lisa could only see their feet under Luther's truck and their hands passing the bottle, through the windows of the cab. Ben was short and stooping and very dark. His face looked almost Chinese and he had a little beard around his mouth and chin. He was still strong, although he was starting to like to talk about how old he was getting. Amelia or Mrs. Denmark would be angry at him most times for drinking, but hog killing was a big party for everybody. He told Lisa once that there was nothing like a drink for a cough and then he told her not to tell her mama. She knew that what he said was true because her mother would give her a spoon of whiskey with sugar in it if she was coughing and sick.

Robert and Jack Lee were blocking out a hog that had already been gutted. Jack cut off the head with a chopping ax, and then used the ax to separate the backbone out from the ribs. The spine came out in one piece, with the stiff little tail still at the end of it. The men began to section up the sides of meat with their knives.

Ben Tyler came down from the parked cars and went over to where the hogs were hanging. He had a foot tub with him, which he set under the nose of one of the hogs. From the back pocket of his overalls he took a long butcher knife, and he threw down the cigarette that was in his mouth. Lisa was watching attentively, standing near the scalding trough.

Ben stood up straight and pushed the round hat he always wore to the back of his head. He put the point of the knife in between the hog's hind legs and pulled it straight down, almost to the big cut on the throat. Then he laid the knife on the scuffed snow beside the tub and parted the opening he had made. A great knot of blue entrails began to roll out of the hog's belly. Ben guided the tangled guts into the tub with his veiny hands. When they were all detached he took out the liver and began to slosh water into the cavity.

Lisa was backing up, watching Ben closely, and without knowing it she touched her thighs to the rim of the scalding trough. When she tried to take the next step she flipped over the edge and into the water. She was so heavily dressed that very little water got to her skin, but it wasn't easy for her to get out. She hadn't opened her mouth, but Ben and Amelia both came running at the sound of the splash.

Ben grabbed her hands and pulled her, scrambling, over the lip of the trough. Amelia began to yell at him before she stopped running.

"Why you can't keep an eye on her? Miz Denmark gone skin us alive over this."

"Reckon I better care her back down to her mama's house."

"I'm gone take her right inside here before she freeze to death." Amelia led Lisa to the cutting table and rubbed some fat on her hands and face. The child didn't seem to be badly burned. Amelia picked her up and carried her over the broken steps of the porch and into the house.

There was no light in the room they entered except for a red glow from an opening in the large cylindrical woodstove which heated the house. The windows were blinded and the room was dark and close. They walked across vague lumps of cloth and invisible clutter; nothing could be seen clearly. Amelia took Lisa's outer clothes off and hung them by the stove to dry. She put Lisa down on a sofa and covered her with a blanket.

Lisa lay quietly and looked at the orange eye of the stove. It was hot in the room and there was a heavy smell of wood smoke and human musk. She imagined being swallowed by an animal. The patch of light shimmered and expanded in her eyes, and Lisa went to sleep.

She woke up again in her bed at home without knowing surely how she had come there. There was moonlight out the window and her mother was sitting at the edge of the bed.

"Mama," she said, "I know how come Benjamin's so black. It's 'cause he works so hard in the dirt and he put his arms up in the pig's belly."

Mrs. Denmark touched her forehead and felt that it was cool. "Don't say that," she said. "It's not polite to Ben, and it isn't true."

Lisa closed her mouth and turned her eyes to the window. She could see the beginning of the road that ran from her house to the hill where the hog killing had been. Now she remembered being carried out of the house in the twilight, when the stars were starting to show. Out in the yard there were dark stains and footprints in the snow, which had been melted by the people's walking and had frozen again. The heads of seven hogs rested on the railing of the porch, all the hair scraped from the dull skin except for the toughest bristles. Their eyes were narrowed or entirely closed, and their jaws were shut in jagged smiles. In the vague December light each face seemed to possess some secret.

· 2 ·

Ben Tyler felt like some piece of scorching wood, walking under the August sun, thinking how the heat might drive him out of his mind. From old habit he wore clothes that covered everything but his hands and face, and now his body could not breathe. The air was still and heavy and it took effort to penetrate it. He had to keep moving, though, to get on with the extra work the drought made for him to do.

All along the barn lot the dirt had hardened and cracked into small octagons and trapezoids. Ben ground powder with his feet, walking on the packed earth. Near an old bathtub which was used as a watering trough a sweaty horse stood, moving only to twitch flies away. Ben passed the tub on his way up the little grade to the barn, and turned the faucet on to refill it. It had not rained for weeks. The pasture was yellowing in the dry heat and the grass seed he had planted on the lawn for Mrs. Denmark had had no chance to sprout.

Mrs. Denmark said it was more important to save the garden than to try to grow grass, so that was how Ben would spend the afternoon. There were sprinklers and hoses in the barn and he would carry them down to the garden to try to keep the ground there moist. Water spilled directly on the plants would boil and scald the leaves, but it would be some help to keep the earth around them from hardening. When he pulled the barn door open it dragged roughly across the small stones fixed in the ground. He needed to raise the hinges.

It was no cooler in the hall of the barn, though the darkness there was a relief to the eyes. Ben's thick shoes sank deeply and coated themselves in the dust of the dirt floor, a much finer powder than the dust outside. He walked up a pair of wooden steps and opened the door to the room where the saddles were kept. The same grit covered the saddles and the shelves that ran along the walls. Ben knelt down and felt in the corners below the lowest shelf for the hosepipes that had been stored there. He pulled out a length of hose and flexed it in his hands to see if the drought and heat had cracked it. The particles that his motion raised glowed in the flat shafts of sunlight which came through the cracks between the boards of the wall.

He tested all the pieces of hose he could find and tied them into coils with bits of baling twine. There were two sprinklers under the shelf that he thought were not broken and he took these out also. His tongue felt rough and swollen, too large for his mouth, and he began to think of how thirsty he was. The dim space of the barn smelled of musty straw and dried horse manure. He wished there would be a breeze.

When he came outside again he saw Lisa walking down the steps from the door of her mother's white house. She walked in the dense shade under the big trees of the yard, watching her feet on the brick path and swinging her hands. The dress she wore was pale blue and hung straight to her calves, unbelted. Looking at her across the bare lot, Ben thought that she seemed to be moving in an improbably cool globe, although he knew it was as hot in the yard as anywhere else.

With the coils of hose slung over his shoulder he walked back to the horse trough and sat down on one of the large pocked stones beside the faucet. He reached for the cup that he kept there, filled it from the tap and drank. When he was halfway down the second cupful he looked back toward the house. Lisa had come to the end of the walk and mounted the low brick wall that ran to the gate of the barn lot. She walked along the top of the wall and climbed the square brick post that met the wire fence enclosing the lot. She stood poised on top of the post, her hands out a little from her sides, and stared away over the drying pasture and wooded hill in the direction of Ben's own house. The hem of her dress and the ends of her hair seemed to flutter slightly, though there was no wind to move them. Ben thought that when he had finished his water he would go over and talk to her a little, before he went to the garden.

In the Tyler house it was dark and sweltering; the windows were small and didn't admit much light or air. Amelia had dressed as lightly as possible in a cotton print skirt, but she felt like her huge body was burning from inside. There were four rooms in the house and each was small and low-ceilinged, so that she always felt cramped. The doors between them were almost too narrow for her to pass through.

The front room with the woodstove seemed unnatural in hot weather, for it was meant to hold heat and keep the air out. There were several layers of wallpaper on the walls, too torn and dirty to be decorative. The paper insulation fixed the heat in the room, as did the ragged stuffed furniture. The room was gray with the dirty light that came through the windows. Amelia walked to the door, pushing aside some litter with her feet: newspapers, part of a child's tea set, and a headless doll. She swung the door open, hoping to start some air moving through the house, and stopped to rest a moment, looking down the concrete steps to the gravel road a few yards away.

The toys belonged to Amelia's granddaughter, Jenny's child. Jenny couldn't get along with the man she was married to so she was staying at home for a while. She had never been able to get along well in life and she hadn't married Prester until the baby was almost born. Now she said he was a no-count and she wouldn't stay at his house anymore. She kept the baby, who was four now, but she didn't seem to understand how to take care of her. So Amelia had to watch over the girl whenever she was here, but today she was with Prester's old mother.

From the time she was a baby Jenny never seemed to have good sense, and she didn't have any head for school. She would often stand and stare blankly like she couldn't hear whatever you were saying to her, but it was not until she grew up to the age of sixteen that she began to have the sickness that makes people holler and fall down. When Mrs. Denmark got to know about the falling down she said for Jenny to be taken to the hospital of Central State. There a doctor told Amelia that Jenny would never be smart, which everyone had already known, and it was also discovered that she had become pregnant. They gave names to the things that were wrong with her but Amelia couldn't remember them after they got home, any more than she had remembered the name of the thing that had been growing on her own brain that other time. Jenny was given a medicine for the falling sickness, but it often seemed that either she did not take it or it did not work.

When Son, so called because he was named for his daddy, came home on leave from the Army, he tried to bring Jenny into the arms of the Lord. For days she had turned her head away when he talked, but when he got her to go to a meeting she became as excited about it as she ever was about anything. Soon she became more devoted than Son had ever been, and she began to go to the meetings where people cry out and speak in unknown tongues, not like the church the Tylers had always belonged to.

It was then, just before Son went back to the Army camp, that Jenny had gone to Prester and got him to marry her. All the family was cheered by this act, and they made the best celebration for her they could. But later it appeared that her life had not really been changed.

Amelia was in the kitchen now, shaking pepper into the pot of pork backbone she was boiling on the electric stove. She felt so hot and bad that it was tiresome to do the smallest things. Some days she couldn't understand what she was working for anymore, when it seemed to take all her efforts just to stay in one place.

Out of all her children only Son had not been a disappointment to everybody. He had gone in that program in the Army where they give you school for nothing. He had a safe job in the service and now he was an officer. Everyone could tell he had a serious mind.

But the other boy, Henry, had never been able to find a straight path for himself. For short stretches he would work and seem to live right, but it always turned out that he would break loose and spend all his money on wickedness. Because of that he never had any job that amounted to much and in the end no one around wanted to hire him anymore. Finally he got angry with them all and declared he would go to New York or Chicago, where he said there was a better life. No one in the family believed he had the money for such a trip and it was not until he had been gone a few days that they began to notice the small things of value that were missing. They never heard from him and he didn't write to them even for money.

Now she couldn't even talk to Benjamin anymore about all the problems. In her heart she still felt that he was a good man but she could never understand how the bad seed had come into the family. She remembered how he was when they both were young, quick and funny and so strong for his size that everyone was amazed by it. These days his mind was no longer clear and he would always think of drinking whiskey and it would be up to her to stop him.

In the bedroom at the front of the house Jenny was still asleep, and she had not undressed yet from coming in the night before. She would often sleep until late in the afternoon, and she never cared to do anything useful. Amelia thought of waking her up, but it seemed there was no reason to. She couldn't think of any direction she herself should move in. She was tired, so tired, and looked forward only to the day when everything would be explained to her. Wiping big drops of sweat from her forehead, she took a step back from the heat of the stove.

Without anyone's knowledge, the malignancy in Amelia's brain had returned and grown to a painful size. As she moved now, it broke apart and swirled forcefully all through her head. The picture that the room made in her eye diminished to the size of a postage stamp and then disappeared completely as she fell across the top of the stove. Her elbow struck the boiling pot, which bounced from the wall to the floor, spilling the meat and the water. The crook of her arm rested on the glowing coil of the stove, and after she had lain there for a while the arm began to char.

In the room by the road Jenny turned over on her back and swung her feet to the floor. She put her head in her hands and rubbed at her eyes for a minute or two. Her mouth was sticky and stale, and she rose and moved toward the kitchen to look for something to drink. She walked a little unsteadily, bumping against the door as she left the room.

There was a little sick smell of burning that met her before she entered the kitchen. When she stepped into the room her eyes grew round and white, and her mouth opened itself and hung waiting. For a moment she stood breathing deeply, and then her hands rose and waved twice in front of her face.

"Oh little Jesus," she said. "Send the demons out of my body." On the last word she threw herself at the floor and rolled there, flailing her arms and legs. Moaning came from her mouth and her spine moved in long violent jerks. A wild sweep of her leg upset a wooden chair, which fell across the door that opened to the back yard. The convulsions of her trunk became stronger and her body thrashed like a snake after it has been hit and before it dies. Her limbs and head were tossed at random by the motion that came from the center of her body, and foam appeared at the edges of her chewing mouth. With each jerk her head slammed soundly against the floor. Gradually the jerks became less frequent, and Jenny lay slackly on her side, knees drawn up toward her chest.

Out in the yard a starling skipped toward the open door in zigzags, picking at the dirt. He hopped onto the edge of the fallen chair and turned his scruffy head sideways to the room. Jenny twitched and raised her head, and the starling flapped sloppily into the air. Jenny clasped the edge of a shelf and raised herself to her feet. She stood and stared at the spilled pot and the massive body humped on the stove. Then she turned and ran out the door, catching her loose shoe on the chair. She rushed into the clumps of buck-bushes and cedars at the edge of the yard, following the straightest way to the Denmark house. Her mouth flew open and she began to cry out, not in grunts as she had before, but in high pure screams. As she moved into the thicket her clothes caught on thorned vines, and she began to tear at the front of her garments with her hands, not slowing her pace.

Lisa stayed standing when Benjamin came over to the post; she moved lightly from foot to foot. She would turn her head to look at him and then look away, back to the hill and the trees. Ben's voice rolled out smoothly, explaining how the heat sapped all the life from him, how the weather didn't give a man a chance, how he was feeling his age. All of this Lisa had heard before, too often to be interested, but she loved to hear the sound of his speaking. She shifted her feet and swung her head in rhythm to the talk. An object detached itself from the trees at the edge of the pasture, and Lisa's head stopped moving. Her eyes sharpened and began to track the object on its path down the hill.

Ben was facing away from the hillside, so he couldn't see the running figure. Lisa kept watching and saw that it was a person, that the person was waving its arms and stumbling as it rushed toward the gate between the field and the lot. As it fumbled with the gate latch Lisa recognized it as a woman. The woman thrust the gate open and ran through, leaving the gate swinging. Her feet, sockless in heavy unlaced boots, beat a cloud of dust from the cracked ground. A twig of bramble hung from the skirt of her dark dress, which was torn in front to disclose white underwear and heaving black skin. Her eyes rolled and her mouth flopped exhaustedly, and it was not until Benjamin turned to look at her that she began to scream again.

Ben turned to follow Lisa's gaze and saw her coming through the gate. He stood quietly, looking toward Jenny's pumping legs as she came on, crying, "Mama done dead, mama dead," over and over, with other sounds that were not words. Lisa looked down at him from the post and he seemed to bend and shrink in her eyes. Then she felt her mother's hands on her shoulders, turning her back to the house, and heard her voice telling her to go back, to go up to her room and wait, to take a nap. Almost frightened now, Lisa hurried away along the wall, looking back over her shoulder to where Mrs. Denmark was speaking, first to Ben,

who was shriveling so small, then to shrieking Jenny, trying
to extract some form of sense from this mad situation. The
scene contracted under the burning sun as Lisa moved
through the green shade into the cool shadows of the house.

· 3 ·

One hog stood half hidden by a drooping branch of a cedar
tree, halfway up the little rise from the shed where they all
were fed. He was white with many black blotches, and was
covered with wet brown mud, which the rainy winter kept
stirred up in the hog lot. The hog and his four brothers of
the litter had churned the mud constantly with their small
heavy feet, so that around the shed it was worked into a
soft gripping paste several inches deep. But up the rise and
back in the lot the ground was firmer, though slick, and
there were rocks and roots to stiffen it. The mud on the
prickly back of the hog beneath the tree was streaked by
the cold morning drizzle.

Inside the feed room Benjamin was sitting on a sack of
shelled corn, stopping to breathe awhile, for he often felt
bad in the mornings now. He took a little drink from the
secret bottle that he had left under the empty sacks. The
room had a small window and with the door shut it was so
dark he could see nothing but shadows. The bottle glinted a
little in the dim light and clanked when he set it down. After
he had replaced it in the hiding place he could hear disturbed mice moving under the sacks. He kept several bottles
now, hidden in the outbuildings, and believed that no one
knew about them. He had told Lisa to wait for him outside
the gate, so she wouldn't see him take his drink.

He heard her voice, clear in the foggy air, saying, "Look,
Benjamin, the hogs are out." He got up slowly to peer out
of the high window, and there was the hog, wrinkling his

long snout. Ben picked up a coffee can from the floor and scooped it half full of corn. He opened the door and went out into the lot, rattling the corn to attract the hogs back to the shed. The hog by the cedar tree stiffened and then bolted, and Ben could see the backs of all five of them through the trees as they ran grunting into the brush. Somehow he must have forgotten to latch the door tight the night before, and Jack Lee and Luther were coming to kill this morning. He knew Mrs. Denmark was going to bite his head off when she found out about this.

Lisa leaned all the way back, supporting herself with a hand on the wire gate, and looked up at the sky. There was nothing to see but the mist drifting and a cover of dull-colored clouds. Light rain fell on her face, and she lowered her head and pulled up the hood of her raincoat. Then she turned around and leaned her back against the gate. She could now see Luther's old battered truck coming unevenly across the rough ground, past the cow barn and toward the hog lot.

The truck pulled up beside the lot fence and Luther got out and let down the tailgate, so that later they could load the hogs and haul them away for cleaning and blocking. Lisa could see that both men had white stubble on their faces, and she smelled liquor when they came near. Each carried a light rifle. Ben had come around to the gate to meet them, bringing his own gun.

Ben scratched the back of his neck while he explained that the hogs had got loose, and Luther answered him, mumbling. Luther and Jack Lee came through the gate and the three of them walked up toward the thicket, with Lisa following at a little distance. The hogs had stopped under some low bushes and they had all turned their heads back to the shed. They tensed as the men came near them but they kept watching and did not run. When the three men raised their rifles a couple of hogs grunted and the group began to swing away. There was a ragged sound of gunfire and squealing as the hogs scattered through the thorn bushes.

One burst out into the clearing and ran to the creek bank behind the shed, where it collapsed, floundering. Ben pursued it, almost falling in the mud which clung to his feet as he tried to run, and as he drew near he pulled the butcher knife from his pocket. When he reached the twitching body he dropped onto his knees, shoved the knife hard into the side of the hog's throat, and made a quick slash all across it. The hog kicked and twisted, and a great rush of fresh blood came out and ran into the creek water. Ben stood up and began to walk back toward the others. Lisa, who had been standing apart, trailed behind him, watching everything sharply.

All of the men were laughing and shouting, excited and out of breath. They came together and leaned on their rifle barrels, trying to get their wind back. Only two hogs had been killed by the shots, and they weren't sure how many might have been hit. They didn't rest long before they spread out into the thicket, holding their guns at their hips. Lisa tried to follow them but she was quickly outdistanced. She slowed to a walk and wandered down near the fence at the far end of the lot.

On a high rocky place there was a hog waiting, partly concealed by gray shoots of thorns. Its nostrils were widened and its long flanks moved heavily with its breath. Lisa was near enough to hear the sound of the breathing from the place where she stood. As she watched the hog there were a couple of quick cracks and she saw two round red holes appear in the hog's dirty hide. She heard a man yelling and the hog squealed and ran at her, scattering rocks on its path down the slope. When it came near her it sheered away and plunged into the creek bed, heading toward the fence. Lisa turned to follow the hog with her eyes and saw it wriggle through a broken water gate and disappear into the woods. She ran along the creek to the fence and scrambled over, then followed the hog among the trees.

The hog had run far ahead of her and she had no idea where it could have gone. She looked on the wet ground for tracks, but there were no clear prints because of the fallen leaves. With her head lowered she moved on into the woods, looking for tracks or traces of blood. These woods were strange to her and they were not on her mother's land, so she knew she should stay near the sound of the creek to be sure of finding her way back again. The noise of running and shooting died away behind her as she went farther into the forest.

Walking, she began to forget about the killing and the hog she was looking for. Around her everything was pleasantly calm. Brown sparrows were hopping on the ground and fluttering in the trees. Above the treetops the sky had cleared of rain clouds, though it was still the color of damp limestone. All along the sky looked flat and even, and Lisa thought she saw a buzzard turning through a gap in the branches. It had not become much lighter.

The creek bent across Lisa's path and as she started to cross it she saw that for several feet the stream was heavily stained with blood. For a moment she thought of the hog she was looking for, but then she remembered the one that had fallen in the water earlier. She was surprised, because she wouldn't have expected all the blood to hang together so far down the creek. She began to follow the red patch as it slipped and wound along the stream.

Lisa was fascinated by the quality of the moving blood, how it seemed to be so much more solid than the water. It floated in many small strands which wove themselves in a complicated matrix, and each strand looked as solid as a piece of fiber. Yet when Lisa put her hand into the water the strands divided around it and became insubstantial. She wondered what blood looked like when it was inside a body, and this thought absorbed her so deeply that she would never have noticed the hog if it had not fallen very near the creek.

It lay dully on its side with its hind feet at the edge of the water. Lisa could see no wounds on it, and she thought they must be on the side against the ground. Its body had not stiffened yet, but the eyes were glazing over. Lisa was glad to have found it, and proud that she knew what needed to be done. Then she realized that she had no knife.

Benjamin climbed over the hog lot fence near the place where Lisa had done so and hurried into the woods. He couldn't clear his mind of the picture of Mrs. Denmark's angry face. It had been bad enough when she saw how the hogs had escaped, but when she learned that Lisa was missing she had become almost too furious to speak.

Luther had told Ben that he thought he had seen the girl going over the fence, and so Ben had a chance to be the first to find her. He felt sure that the child would have the sense to stay near the creek, for she had lived around the woods all her life. He moved as fast as he could along the bank, afraid to call her name because there might be no answer. His fear was about to break out in a shout when he came around a turn in the stream and saw her.

She was sitting on the ribs of the warm dead hog, with her hands holding each other in her lap. She wasn't looking in his direction, but away through the trees. At once he saw that she was unhurt and no terrible harm had been done, and his head throbbed with the relief. The thrill of safety made him feel young again, and he ran up to touch her as she turned to look at him. He lifted her under the shoulders and stared into her face, and her eyes were clear and empty as the sky.

The
Naked
Lady

for Alan Lequire

THIS IS A THING that happened before Monroe started maken the heads, while he was still maken the naked ladies.

Monroe went to the college and it made him crazy for a while like it has done to many a one.

He about lost his mind on this college girl he had. She was just a little old bit of a thing and she talked like she had bugs in her mouth and she was just nothen but trouble. I never would of messed with her myself.

When she thrown him over we had us a party to take his mind off it. Monroe had these rooms in a empty mill down by the railroad yard. He used to make his scultures there and we was both liven there too at the time.

We spent all the money on whiskey and beer and everbody we known come over. When it got late Monroe appeared to drop a stitch and went to thowin bottles at the walls. This caused some people to leave but some other ones stayed on to help him I think.

I had a bad case of drunk myself. A little before sunrise I crawled off and didn't wake up till up in the afternoon. I had a sweat from sleepin with clothes on. First thing I seen when I opened my eyes was this big old rat setten on the floor side the mattress. He had a look on his face like he was wonderen would it be safe if he come over and took a bite out of my leg.

It was the worst rats in that place you ever saw. I never saw nothin to match em for bold. If you chunked somethin at em they would just back off a ways and look at you mean. Monroe had him this tin sink that was full of plaster from the scultures and ever night these old rats would mess in it. In the mornin you could see they had left tracks goen places you wouldnt of believed somethin would go.

We had this twenty-two pistol we used to shoot em up with but it wasnt a whole lot of good. You could hit one of these rats square with a twenty-two and he would go off with it in him and just get meaner. About the only way to kill one was if you hit him spang in the head and that needs you to be a better shot than I am most of the time.

We did try a box of them exploden twenty-twos like what that boy shot the President with. They would take a rat apart if you hit him but if you didnt they would bounce around the room and bust up the scultures and so on.

It happened I had put this pistol in my pocket before I went to bed so Monroe couldnt get up to nothin silly with it. I taken it out slow and thew down on this rat that was looken me over. Hit him in the hindquarter and he went off and clamb a pipe with one leg draggen.

I sat up and saw the fluorescents was on in the next room thew the door. When I went in there Monroe was messen around one of his sculture stands.

Did you get one, he said.

Winged him, I said.

That aint worth much, Monroe said. He off somewhere now plotten your doom.

I believe the noise hurt my head more'n the slug hurt that rat, I said. Is it any whiskey left that you know of?

Let me know if you find some, Monroe said. So I went to looken around. The place was nothin but trash and it was glass all over the floor.

I might of felt worse sometime but I dont just remember when it was, I said.

They's coffee, Monroe said.

I went in the other room and found a half of a pint of Heaven Hill between the mattress and the wall where I must of hid it before I tapped out. Pretty slick for drunk as I was. I taken it in to the coffee pot and mixed half and half with some milk in it for the sake of my stomach.

Leave me some, Monroe said. I hadnt said a word, he must of smelt it. He tipped the bottle and took half what was left.

The hell, I said. What you maken anyway?

Naked lady, Monroe said.

I taken a look and it was this shape of a woman setten on a mess of clay. Monroe made a number of these things at the time. Some he kept and the rest he thrown out. Never could tell the difference myself.

Thats all right, I said.

No it aint, Monroe said. Soon's I made her mouth she started in asken me for stuff. She wants new clothes and she wants a new car and she wants some jewry and a pair of Italian shoes.

And if I make her that stuff, Monroe said, I know she's just goen to take it out looken for some other fool. I'll set here all day maken stuff I dont care for and she'll be out just riden and riden.

Dont make her no clothes and she cant leave, I said.

She'll whine if I do that, Monroe said. The whole time you was asleep she been fussen about our relationship.

You know the worst thing, Monroe said. If I just even thought about maken another naked lady I know she would purely raise hell.

Why dont you just make her a naked man and forget it, I said.

Why dont I do this? Monroe said. He whopped the naked lady with his fist and she turned into a flat clay pancake, which Monroe put in a plastic bag to keep soft. He could hit a good lick when he wanted. I hear this is common among scultures.

Dont you feel like doen somethin, Monroe said.

I aint got the least dime, I said.

I got a couple dollars, he said. Lets go see if it might be any gas in the truck.

They was some. We had this old truck that wasnt too bad except it was slow to start. When we once got it goen we drove over to this pool hall in Antioch where nobody didnt know us. We stayed awhile and taught some fellers that was there how to play rotation and five in the side and some other games that Monroe was good at. When this was over with we had money and I thought we might go over to the Ringside and watch the fights. This was a bar with a ring in the middle so you could set there and drink and watch people get hurt.

We got in early enough to take seats right under the ropes. They was an exhibition but it wasnt much and Monroe started in on this little girl that was setten by herself at the next table.

Hey there Juicy Fruit, he said, come on over here and get somethin real good.

I wouldnt, I told him, haven just thought of what was obvious. Then this big old hairy thing came out from the back and sat down at her table. I known him from a poster out front. He was champion of some kind of karate and had come all the way up from Atlanta just to beat somebody to death and I didnt think he would care if it was Monroe. I got Monroe out of there. I was some annoyed with him because I would have admired to see them fights if I could do it without bein in one myself.

So Monroe said he wanted to hear music and we went some places where they had that. He kept after the girls but they wasnt any trouble beyond what we could handle. After while these places closed and we found us a little railroad bar down on Lower Broad.

It wasnt nobody there but the pitifulest band you ever heard and six bikers, the big fat ugly kind. They wasnt the

Hell's Angels but I believe they would have done until some come along. I would of left if it was just me.

Monroe played pool with one and lost. It wouldnt of happened if he hadnt been drunk. He did have a better eye than me which may be why he is a sculture and I am a second-rate pool player.

How come all the fat boys in this joint got on black leather jackets? Monroe hollered out. Could that be a new way to lose weight?

The one he had played with come bellyen over. These boys like to look you up and down beforehand to see if you might faint. But Monroe hooked this one side of the head and he went down like a steer in the slaughterhouse. This didnt make me as happy as it might of because it was five of em left and the one that was down I thought apt to get up shortly.

I shoved Monroe out the door and told him to go start the truck. The band had done left already. I thown a chair and I thown some other stuff that was layen around and I ducked out myself.

The truck wasnt started yet and they was close behind. It was this old four-ten I had under the seat that somebody had sawed a foot off the barrel. I taken it and shot the sidewalk in front of these boys. The pattern was wide on account of the barrel bein short like it was and I believe some of it must of hit all of em. It was a pump and took three shells and I kept two back in case I needed em for serious. But Monroe got the truck goen and we left out of there.

I was some mad at Monroe. Never said a word to him till he parked outside the mill. It was a nice moon up and thowin shadows in the cab when the headlights went out. I turned the shotgun across the seat and laid it into Monroe's ribs.

What you up to? he said.

You might want to die, I said, but I dont believe I want to go with you. I pumped the gun to where you could hear the shell fallen in the chamber.

If that's what you want just tell me now and I'll save us both some trouble.

It aint what I want, Monroe said.

I taken the gun off him.

I dont know what I do want, Monroe said.

Go up there and make a naked lady and you feel better, I told him.

He was messen with clay when I went to sleep but that aint what he done. He set up a mirror and done a head of himself instead. I taken a look at the thing in the mornin and it was a fair likeness. It looked like it was thinkin about all the foolish things Monroe had got up to in his life so far.

That same day he done one of me that was so real it even looked like it had a hangover. Ugly too but that aint Monroe's fault.

He is makin money with it now.

How we finally fixed them rats was we brought on a snake. Monroe was the one to have the idea. It was a good-sized one and when it had just et a rat it was as big around as your arm. It didnt eat more than about one a week but it appeared to cause the rest of em to lay low.

You might say it was as bad to have snakes around as rats but at least it was only one of the snake.

The only thing was when it turned cold the old snake wanted to get in the bed with you. Snakes aint naturally warm like we are and this is how come people think they are slimy, which is not the truth when you once get used to one.

This old snake just comes and goes when the spirit moves him. I aint seen him in a while but I expect he must be still around.

Monkey
Park

for Carroll Murray Jones Lofty

AT FIVE O'CLOCK in the afternoon the light comes in yellow across the brown curling paint at the edge of the window sill and makes the stained white walls of the kitchen glow golden, makes the tired enamel at the bottom of the sink look like old ivory. Carolee's just back from her job, she's a waitress in a lunch place this month, and she's in a pretty good mood. She finishes off the dishes from breakfast, and the hot water is pleasant over her hands, the last clot of suds moves toward the drain and Carolee flicks it away with a worn-out sponge that's shaped like an apple. She watches the afternoon light on the wall and it makes her feel warm and electric, like she wants something to happen.

Then something does happen. Carolee hears this awful noise, like a cross between a chain saw and a jackhammer, it's getting closer and closer and finally it comes around the corner of the house and stops under the kitchen windows. Carolee looks out through the vines that are crawling along the window panes and sees that the noise belongs to a big old wreck of a car, long and gray with blood-red flecks on it, like an enormous sickly shark. The car coughs and groans and chokes and dies, and the driver gets out and bangs the door and it's Perry. Perry walks around the tail fins of the car and starts up the cracked concrete walk to the back door, and Carolee can even hear his feet rustling over the tough little weeds that grow up between the cracks, which means that Perry is definitely here.

Oh hell, Carolee thinks, but she can't not be glad to see Perry, so she dries her hands on the dishtowel and dabs at the water spots on her jeans. Then she flips her hair back away from her eyes and goes around to the back door to let Perry in.

"So what are you doing back in town," Carolee says.

"Shrimpers in Bayou La Batre," Perry says.

"Oh," Carolee says. "But this isn't Bayou La Batre, you know."

"I know," Perry says. "I quit."

"Well come in the kitchen and drink some beer," Carolee says. So they go in the kitchen and Carolee gets out a bottle of Stroh's and pours it into two glasses. They sit down beside the table in there, which has an enamel top with black speckles in it, and they don't say anything. Carolee lights a Lucky Strike and pushes the pack over to Perry and they smoke and watch the smoke whirling and spinning across the wide shafts of orange light in the kitchen. After a few minutes or so Carolee gets up and takes another beer from the fridge and pours it into the two glasses. Then she stands there with her fingers touching the table.

There's a little green tattoo smudged on the back of Perry's dirty pale hand, though she can't quite tell what it is. It looks like it could be initials or something, but it seems that Perry has tried to get rid of it, so it really isn't readable at all. Well, Perry doesn't look like someone that ought to have a tattoo. He doesn't even look much like someone that ought to work on a shrimp boat. He's little and light and not very strong looking, though he has a nice enough face and all that. He's got messy black hair and dark eyes and the sun never tans him or even burns him somehow, he just stays pale and grubby all the time. All of a sudden Carolee is afraid that

Perry is going to say, "Aren't you glad to see me?" so she wills him not to say this, and he doesn't.

Instead Perry gets down on the floor and lies on his side with his knees drawn up to his belt buckle and his hands cocked in front of him like the paws of a begging dog.

"I have now metamorphosed into a shrimp," Perry announces. "I've looked into too many nets. I've seen too many little gray squiggles. I'm done for. I am a shrimp. I have a pointy nose and little feelers and no bones. I eat tiny garbage all over the big wide sea."

"Oh God," says Carolee. "Shut up and get off the floor."

Perry gets up and wiggles his fingers in front of his face.

"I will now clasp you in my shrimply embrace," he says. He makes a dive at Carolee but she dodges out of the way, and Perry turns around in the corner of the kitchen and puts his hands back in his pockets. That's when Carolee notices the green bruise healing around his left eye socket. It almost looks like make-up, only there's a line of an old cut there too, and Carolee wonders if he really did quit the boat or if somebody just pitched him head first onto the docks one day.

"Well, I do smell like a shrimp, anyway," Perry says. "You can admit that."

"You smell like a lot of shrimp," Carolee says. Then she stalks over to Perry and gives him a quick hard hug, pushes him away and goes back to the windows, but the light is fading now, so she turns back around and half sits on the sill. Perry has enough sense not to be grinning.

"I have money," Perry says. "I have shrimp in the car. Shrimp for supper. Eh?"

"All right," Carolee says then. "Go upstairs and take a shower."

"Maybe I should bring the shrimp in," Perry says.

"I'll get the shrimp," Carolee says. "Go on and get in the shower. I'll bring you up a towel in a minute."

There's a window in the bathroom tucked up under the eaves and Perry can look out over the tar-papered kitchen roof and see Carolee going out to the car, walking with quick reedy movements. Perry watches her peering into the ruined interior, finding the cooler and swinging it up over her narrow chest. She steps out from the car and closes the door with a brisk backward kick. The cooler is heavy, Perry knows, but Carolee stands there for a minute holding it, looking up at the window under the roof. Perry can't see her face too well at this distance, but he knows perfectly well what it looks like, freckles splayed over the urgent birdlike features, the sandy hair that keeps drifting over her eyes. Carolee shifts her glance and marches into the house, and Perry dunks his head back under the shower stream. He hears the back door slam closed behind Carolee, over the running water, and he lets water run in and out of his ears, thinking how her eyes look when they catch the sudden light beams in the kitchen: translucent, glowing, oceanic green.

Then Perry picks up a piece of soap from the tray in the shower and squeezes it until he's got enough lather to wash his hair with and when he's done that he rubs the soap lump all over himself till all the fish slime is gone. Carolee cracks the bathroom door and hangs a red towel over the key that sits in the lock of it.

"Jesus, Perry," she says. "There's water all over the floor. There's a shower curtain on the shower, you know."

"I wanted to look out the window," says Perry. "I'll clean it all up when I get out."

"You better," Carolee says. Then she bangs the door shut, hard enough to rattle the key in the lock, but the towel keeps on hanging there.

Carolee even goes out and finds Perry's old duffel bag in the trunk of the car, so when Perry has finished his shower and dried up the floor he finds clean clothes waiting for him outside the bathroom. So Perry puts these clean clothes on and goes downstairs, rubbing his hair around with the dripping red towel. He goes into the kitchen where Carolee is. Perry's eyes are red and stinging from the soap that got in them and the evening air feels cool on his wrists and the back of his neck.

"Is Alphonse around?" Perry says.

"He's not in the house," says Carolee. "He's in town, all right, if that's what you mean."

"Oh," says Perry, and he drops the wet towel over the back of a chair. "I saw Art in Bayou La Batre. He told me that Alphonse was thinking about a two-month job in Brazil."

"He decided not to take that job," Carolee says. "He's still working for Rock City." Alphonse is a solid blond cheerful man with a degree in Building and Construction. He inspects constructions while they are being built. That is his profession. Sunset is over and the light in the kitchen is now a subaqueous gray.

"I don't see how you can be married to someone named Alphonse," Perry says.

"You don't have to see it," Carolee says. "It isn't your problem." Perry lights another one of Carolee's Luckies and doesn't think of anything else to say. But cigarettes do taste good after showers. Carolee rolls up the dishtowel and pops it toward Perry's limp collar.

"Besides, it's not his fault he's named Alphonse," she says. "His family is French from New Orleans."

"I don't believe that for a minute," Perry says. "I think his family is crazy is all." Carolee wraps the dishtowel around her wrist and turns to look out the window.

"It's getting dark in here," she says.

"All right," Perry says. "How do we do the shrimp?"

"Boil them?"

"Fry them?"

"Too much trouble."

"Do them in butter, no bread."

"Still have to clean them."

"I'll do it," Perry says. He goes out to the car and stands beside it, finishing the nub of the cigarette. The light snaps on at the kitchen windows, and Perry drops the butt and grinds it carefully into the dry red dirt. It's getting very dark now and the light is blue and up above the scrubby pine tops Perry can see the evening star. He reaches into the glove compartment through the open car window and gets out a red plastic shrimp peeler and carries it back to the house.

"Maybe you better not start yet," Carolee says. "Alphonse might be back to supper, only I don't know when."

"That's all right," Perry says, shrugging. "I'll just clean them now and put them in the fridge." Carolee goes to help him but Perry waves her away.

"Make sauce or something," he says. "There's only one peeler anyway." So Carolee sits at the table and watches him cleaning the shrimp with his deft bony hands, pushing the peeler from neck to tail, flicking the shells onto a newspaper and the shrimp into a bowl. Then the telephone rings in the living room and Carolee goes in there and picks it up. There's no light on in there and only a little dimness seeping in at the windows by now.

Carolee comes back in the kitchen.

"Alphonse is working late," she says. "Alphonse is having dinner with a business acquaintance. He wants us to meet him at the Wheel at ten."

"Fine," says Perry, slinging shrimp around. "I'm hungry right now, anyway."

"He wants to talk to you," Carolee says. "He's still on the phone." The peeler clicks into the sink and Perry walks out of the kitchen and picks up the telephone, which is sitting on one of those little round tables with a pole lamp sticking up through the middle. Perry puts the receiver to his ear and starts switching the light on and off. Carolee notices he forgot to wash his hands, so he's leaving shrimp goo all over the telephone and hanging sand veins on the pull chain of the lamp.

"Hey there good buddy," Alphonse says. "Good to hear you, good to hear you're back in town. Yeah, Carolee tells me you're back in town, so how're you doing, old buddy?"

"The same," Perry says. He pulls at the light chain. Alphonse's voice feels like it is right there in the room and slapping Perry on the back.

"Hey, sure, I know what you mean, hey. Nothing too much changes, does it? Naw, nothing too much changes. Hey, but I hope you'll be hanging around some this time, no trouble to us to put you up, got plenty of room and all. So hang around a few days, old buddy, maybe we'll take off and go fishing."

"Thanks, Alphonse," Perry says. "Thanks for the invite. I don't quite know how long I'll be around, though. I don't exactly know what's going to happen."

"Well that's fine, old buddy, that's just fine," Alphonse says. "I know just exactly what you mean. But anyway, I'll see you tonight, you're coming on up to the Wheel tonight, with Carolee, aren't you, right?"

"I'll be there," Perry says. "Take it easy, Alphonse. Until ten."

Perry hangs up the telephone and goes back to the kitchen, and Carolee goes in the living room and starts cleaning off the phone and the light stand. She cleans them very carefully so there won't be any fish smell and by the time she gets through the shrimp are already getting pink and rosy in the skillet that Perry has put them in, with onion and butter and a trace of garlic, and the shrimp smell very good indeed.

"We don't need any sauce anyway," Perry says. "These

are just right how they are." So they both sit down at the
table with salt and pepper and shrimp and beer, and Carolee
feels good because eating something this good makes her
feel purely happy. Then the shrimp have all been eaten and
Carolee gets up and opens another bottle of beer. But Perry
covers his glass with his hand.

"No more right now," he says. He looks up at the clock
on the wall and it's still only seven.

"I got a little number out in the car," Perry says. "You
want to do a little number, maybe? Carolee?"

So then they do the little number, standing out by the car
in the vague starlight, and then they go in the house and
drink a lot of water to ward off the cotton mouth. They
go in the living room and sit on the sofa and Carolee plays
Billie Holiday and then Hank Williams, and then Billie
Holiday again. The songs are pained and lonely, but Carolee
feels fine and free and floating, and there is no light in the
room except for the tip of one of Carolee's cigarettes that
Perry is smoking, and Carolee's elbow is touching Perry's
elbow, and Perry's knee is touching Carolee's knee, and
Carolee jumps off the sofa and runs up the stairs to her bedroom. Then she comes back to the banister and calls down
the stairs.

"Come on up here, Perry," she says. "I got a real stage
make-up kit now, I'll make you a face."

Then Perry climbs up to Carolee's bedroom and she makes
him put out the cigarette, and she lights a candle and sets it
up in a saucer on the floor. Then she puts the make-up box
on the floor near the candle and works on Perry for a while
with the things in the box, and she criticizes him whenever
he twitches. Perry wants to look at himself when she's done,
but Carolee says no. She scoots the candle over to the bottom
of the full-length mirror on the closet door and crouches
there, working on her own face for a long time while Perry

sits in the corner feeling foolish and sticky. Then Carolee reaches behind her and takes Perry by the wrist and pulls him over so their faces are together over the candle and they're looking at themselves in the mirror.

Perry's face is simple and harsh, his skin is whiter than ever now, and he's got black lips and black slashes over his eyes and that's all, it makes him look like a mime or a ghost. Carolee's face is more subtle and dangerous, she's lengthened her nose and raised her cheekbones and added some colors here and there. She looks as deathly as Perry does, also beautiful and fierce and disdainful.

"That's scary," Perry says, and he starts when he sees the lips of his mask moving. "You look scary, Carolee."

"Do you like it?" Carolee says.

"I don't know if I like it," Perry says. "Oh, you did a good job, all right." In the mirror Perry sees Carolee turn her head and look at him hard over the candle, so he has to turn and look at her too.

"Don't look like that," Perry says.

Carolee keeps looking.

"It's ten already," Perry says.

So then they get up and go in the bathroom and Carolee finds some cold cream to take the faces off with, and they wash the faces off with this, standing side by side over the sink. When that's done they go down and outside to the car, and Perry arranges some of his clothes over the seat so the springs won't stick into Carolee. Perry turns the key and nothing happens at all so he gets out and digs around under the hood and the car starts like a bomb going off. Perry presses a button on the steering column and the car begins to crawl backward down the gravel drive to the street. Then he presses another button and the car begins to move forward. It still sounds like a bomb going off.

"Like the car?" Perry yells to Carolee. "It's got a push-button transmission, the latest thing in cars."

"I guess so," Carolee says. "It makes a hell of a lot of noise."

"That's a special option on this car," Perry says. "It saves having to make conversation."

So they don't make any conversation until Perry has parked the car outside the Wheel, which is something like a cross between a nice little neighborhood bar and a roadhouse. It gets its name from a big old wooden wagon wheel that hangs over the door, and Alphonse is standing to the left of this wheel when Perry and Carolee arrive. Alphonse has a seersucker jacket stretched across his big shoulders, with a lot of pens in the top pocket, and he keeps looking this way and that until Carolee calls to him. Then he walks over to meet them, gives Carolee a peck on the cheek, and squeezes Perry's hand so hard that Perry makes a face. So they all go into the Wheel.

They sit down in a row at the bar and Perry buys everybody a mixed drink, only Carolee just takes a beer. Perry and Alphonse are sitting together and Alphonse tells Perry all his new jokes, and Carolee doesn't listen too closely to this, because Alphonse's new jokes are not new to Carolee. She looks around the Wheel and thinks that it's changed quite a bit since she was a teenager, when all there was to the Wheel was three-legged chairs on a sawdust floor with beer and pool and the odd knife fight. Now there's varnished pine panels all over the walls, and the chairs and bar stools were designed by someone, and there's a big leather cushion along the edge of the bar, which keeps your elbows from getting sore. But the rednecks are still there with their girls and big cars, even if they do have on long hair and satin shirts now, and they still start fights all over the pool tables, even though they have nicer cues to bash each other with these days.

So Carolee sits there and thinks all these things, and she listens to the juke box with one ear and hears Alphonse talking and Perry laughing with the other. Pretty soon Perry buys another round of drinks and Perry and Alphonse start to play an electronic game that they have in the Wheel now. The bartender brings a little box over to Perry and Alphonse, and Perry and Alphonse push buttons on this box, and all sorts of stuff begin to go on on a big lighted screen over the bar: a picture of a man with a gun shoots little lights at pictures of geese, and points are scored from this somehow. Alphonse beats the hell out of Perry at this game, because Perry has never been any good at games of this kind, and after Alphonse has beaten him a few times Perry asks Alphonse to go and shoot pool.

Alphonse beats Perry at pool too, but not so badly, and by now Alphonse is drunk enough to start telling his jokes all over again, and Perry keeps laughing at the jokes and buying more drinks. Perry is acting like everybody's rich uncle, he keeps buying all the drinks and won't let Alphonse buy even one round, and Perry even keeps giving Carolee handfuls of quarters to go play the juke box with. So Carolee plays things on the juke box and she sits at the bar and drinks her beers, and Perry and Alphonse come stand beside her stool and talk to her between shots on the pool table. Everyone's having a wonderful time, and Carolee herself is feeling no pain, until Perry comes over and recites one of Alphonse's jokes to her in such a way that the joke does not seem funny at all.

But Perry has to go make a shot right away, so Carolee doesn't have time to react because Alphonse comes over instead, and Carolee sees that Alphonse is now so drunk that he needs a big piece of the bar to hold himself up with, though he still seems to be winning the pool games. Then Carolee looks over at Perry and notices that he doesn't seem to be drunk at all, though he's been drinking as much as anybody and probably more. Well, Perry has always been like that, he drinks himself drunk and then he drinks himself sober again, only tonight there seems to be something deliberate and scientific about the way he is doing it, and Carolee might wonder what he is cooking, only it seems to be too much trouble, so she gets another beer and forgets about it. Then it's the last call, and then they turn up the house lights and unplug the juke box and start sweeping the floor, and then the only people left in the Wheel are Perry and Alphonse and Carolee.

Perry looks dead sober under the bright lights that are on now, and he takes the cue from Alphonse, who is weaving just a tiny bit, and then Perry runs the table even though this game just started, and then he slams the cue back in the rack. Alphonse's eyes bug out a little at this, and Carolee herself feels suddenly sober, but that turns out not to be entirely true when she gets up onto her feet. Then they are all standing out on the curb, and the taillights of the last jacked-up car are drifting down the highway away from the Wheel, and Alphonse and Perry are on either side of Carolee with their arms linked through her elbows.

"Let's go do something," Perry says. "I feel like doing something."

"It's late," Carolee says. "There's no place open now."

"We can go to the monkey park," Perry says. "Let's go to the monkey park."

The monkey park is in Opelika, which is the next little town down the road, so they all get in the front of the big gray car, with Carolee in the middle. Alphonse has a brand-new Volvo he'd be happy to drive, but Alphonse doesn't know the way and Perry wants to drive himself, so now Alphonse is shifting around on the ragged seat trying to find a spot with no springs sticking out.

"This is some car you got, old buddy," Alphonse says. "You going to customize it? Hey?"

"I like it how it is," Perry says. Then he starts the motor and it drowns out everything.

But when they get on the highway the car goes into some kind of cruising gear and shuts up considerably, and then even when Perry slows it down to go along the quiet little streets of Opelika it still doesn't seem to be making very much noise. Carolee looks out down the streets and thinks of the people asleep in the little white houses on either side, and the car floats along so softly that she doesn't really notice when it slips off the road and stops.

Then Perry gets out and clicks his door shut and Carolee and Alphonse get out on the other side and stretch their stiffening legs. The stars are out and fairly bright but it's still too dark to see faces. There's a little rise up from the roadside and when they get to the top of this they are looking down a long gentle slope, the edge of a deep basin full of trees. At the bottom of the basin, in a clearing there, is a thing that looks like a very big birdbath.

So Perry starts running down the slope toward the birdbath, and Carolee and Alphonse follow him down slowly, Alphonse stumbling just a little. When they get down there it is plain that the thing is not a birdbath at all, though Carolee knows this already, in any case. It's a green metal saucer that sits on a green metal post, and in between there is a ring of ball bearings, so that when Perry gives the saucer a little light push it starts spinning and keeps going for more than a minute.

"I love this thing," Perry says softly. "I think about it all the time when I'm on the boat."

Then Perry stops the coasting saucer with his hand and climbs into it. He sits there with his feet braced on the rim.

"Give me a push," he says, and Carolee takes hold of the rim of the saucer and runs around and around with it till she feels dizzy herself, and then she steps away from it, stands still and breathes hard. Perry freezes in the saucer and stares straight out, and Carolee and Alphonse are braided into the whirling trees so thoroughly that Perry can't pick them out at all, and Perry can't pick anything else out either because everything has blended and flattened itself into one continuous streaming ribbon of vision. Then Perry rolls over onto his back and closes his eyes and tucks up his legs like an embryo. He can feel all the liquor he drank shrinking away until it disappears altogether and only Perry is left there alone with a cold clear mind, solid and calm and perfectly stationary, while the whole rest of the world shrieks by all around him. When Perry opens his eyes again he is looking up into the waning moon that has just risen, and the white light burns a big circle at the top of Perry's sky, and Perry watches the circle until it fragments itself into twelve moons and then six moons and then only two or three, so Perry sits up again, and now he can see a few Alphonses and Carolees flashing by. The saucer stops coasting and Perry gets out.

Then Carolee comes over and gets into the saucer. Perry runs with it until it's spinning fast and then he dodges out to the side. When he turns back around he can't see Carolee because she's lying down flat in the dish, and she stays down for a long time. When the saucer begins to slow down some Carolee sits up and moves toward the edge. Carolee's eyes are open wide and full of the light of the moon, but to Perry she looks like she's in a trance, so deep he thinks she may never come out of it. The dish holds its speed for quite a long time, and Perry begins to wonder if Carolee may not stay there forever, whirling and dreaming and rotating across his line of sight as evenly as his own pulse. But Carolee stretches her foot to the ground and stops it. She gets out of the dish and stands there beside it looking down at her feet.

"Well, Alphonse," Perry says.

"I don't know," Alphonse says.

"You're going to love it, old buddy," Perry says.

"Go on, Alphonse," Carolee says.

Alphonse climbs heavily into the saucer.

"What do I do?" he says.

"It doesn't much matter," Carolee says. "Just keep some of your weight on the center."

So Alphonse gets himself settled in, and Perry and Carolee push him together, until the saucer is going so fast that Carolee can't keep up with it. "That's enough," Carolee says, stepping away, but Perry doesn't hear her, or anyway he doesn't stop. The saucer is going so fast now that Carolee can't see Alphonse at all, and she wonders if he has been whirled away into nothingness, and after a while she can hardly see Perry anymore either. But finally Perry breaks apart from the saucer and runs away from it in a long crooked line, stopping himself on a tree about halfway up the slope. Perry stands there and leans on the tree while the saucer hisses and whirls on its bearings. It's a long time before the saucer seems to slow down at all, and Perry straightens up and stands near the tree as still and silent as if he were a tree himself. Then the breeze starts to blow the treetops together, and the branches sound almost like distant applause, and there is enough moonlight for Carolee and Perry to see each other's faces across the top of the hurtling saucer.

Eventually the saucer does slow down and stop, and something begins to move around inside of it, and this something is Alphonse. Alphonse gets out and starts walking around, only he can't seem to find anybody, he can't even seem to bump into a tree. He wanders around in big sloppy circles with his hands pressed over the top of his face. Then Perry goes over to him and takes him by the arm, whispers in his ear and leads him up the slope into the shadows. Carolee hears all sorts of strange noises coming from there, and she hears Perry's voice as steady and soothing as the night breeze, and after a while Perry comes back by himself.

"Alphonse is sleeping," Perry says, walking toward Carolee. "Alphonse is taking a nap for a while."

"Is he okay?" Carolee says.

"He's just fine," Perry says, still coming on. "He just felt like going to sleep for a while." Perry doesn't stop coming and Carolee can't think of any more questions, so she turns around and starts walking the same way Perry is, walking rather quickly in order to keep ahead of Perry. Then it occurs to her that they are going toward the monkey cage, so then she has something to say.

"Let's go and look at the monkeys," Carolee says, and Perry doesn't say anything at all.

Then Carolee is standing in front of the monkey cage, which is no bigger than an elevator in an office building, and Carolee thinks that the monkeys would probably look pretty shabby in daylight, but by night they seem mysterious and alluring. There's five or six or seven of them, all about the size of five-year-old children, but they're slender and graceful and their movements around the cage seem polished and decorous. The monkeys have fan-shaped puffs of hair around their eyes, and they have long plumed tails. A couple of monkeys come to the front of the cage and gaze at Carolee with what seems to be wisdom and compassion, and a couple more climb up to the top and hang by their feet, to see what Carolee looks like upside down.

Then all the monkeys chitter together and turn their backs and the two at the top drop to the bottom and start combing and stroking each other's fur. Two monkeys come back to the front and reach out through the wires of the cage, and one monkey points a long black finger at Perry.

So then Carolee notices that Perry has caught up with her and in fact he's been there for quite some time, with one hand gripping her on the waist and the other one stroking her hair over and over. Carolee notices now, but she doesn't do anything about it just yet, she just stands there stiffly with both hands holding on to the rail that someone has put up around the cage to keep her from being able to reach her fingers in where the monkeys could bite them. Perry nuzzles her neck and starts whispering into one of her ears, and Carolee doesn't listen to the things that he says, she listens to the monkeys clucking instead, but the monkeys are beginning to look very misty and far away.

"Just stop it," Carolee says. "You might as well just stop it."

"But why —"

"Stop it."

"But I —"

"Stop."

Then Perry stops and even moves a little away from Carolee, only dropping his hand over hers on the rail. The monkeys chitter and clutch at each other and climb up and down all over the cage.

"Where do you think they come from?" Perry says.

"I think they've always been here," Carolee says.

"You think they like it in Opelika," Perry says.

"I don't think they care," Carolee says.

By the time the next silence is over Carolee can see chinks of daylight in the night sky. She looks at the monkeys and they do look worse in the strengthening daylight. The monkeys are all combing and stroking each other again.

"You know why they do that way," Carolee says. "They're just picking salt off of each other's skins."

"You didn't have to say that," Perry says.

"Yes I did," Carolee says. But she lets her hand turn itself over and take hold of Perry's.

"All right, you did then," Perry says. "I have to drive down to New Orleans this morning, because Art says he'll get me a job on a rig." Carolee says nothing to that.

"I'll send you all some postcards," Perry says. "Probably I'll even be back sometime." Carolee doesn't say anything to that either, but she also doesn't let go of Perry's hand, so they just stand there and look into the monkey cage, and they don't say anything to each other at all until the sun tips its rim over the edge of the basin and they hear Alphonse calling to them through the trees.

Triptych II

◆

· I ·

THE PEACOCK DIED at last on the roof of the barn. Two other cocks made up their minds to run him off or kill him. They killed him.

It occurred in the spring, mating season and the time when the birds' feathers are most glorious. All three were bright and beautiful when they stalked each other in the morning damp grass, under the trees and through patches of sunlight. Their necks were sinuous and brilliant blue, and golden scales were on their backs. Behind each trailed a hundred blue and green iridescent blind eyes. Eventually a number of these eye feathers were broken, and red beads began to form on the one cock's back.

They fought on the ground, rushing each other, screeching and flapping into the air, to strike at the head with their spurs. Presently they routed the lone cock into the trees and flew heavily after him from branch to branch. On the ridge of the barn he was caught with a lucky spike that pierced through his little eye to his brain. The other two dropped off the roof and scuffed up dust in the barn lot. There were no more battles that season.

The dead peacock lay loosely on a flat place on the tin roof. The sun scorched him and he stank, but he was too high up for the smell to bother anyone. His flesh came apart and the feathers blew to the ground. After a while, everything but his bones was gone, and they whitened and made a crisp pale hieroglyphic on the dirty roof. The wind broke up that pattern, and there was nothing left then, only a lighter patch on the roof, where the sun had not struck while the body lay there.

· 2 ·

Sunlight passing through the window made stripes on Mr. Eliot, asleep in his black wooden bed. He scrubbed his face across the pillow and turned away from the light. Until he was fully awake he wouldn't remember that he was old. Dreaming, he might be anybody.

When he got up, though, he felt the mound high on his back twisting his shoulders down and forcing his head to stick out like a turtle's head. He'd had a slight hunch as a young man and had a bad one now, crippling. His skin was the color of a cave fish. Still, Mr. Eliot could laugh at the way he looked when he passed the mirror on the way to the window. He knew what he ought not to take seriously.

There was a Baptist college across the street from his window, red, square, and new looking. It hadn't been there as long as the other buildings on the street, mostly huge dank stone houses. Yards tended to be messy and the sidewalks were cracked, and the grassy islands in the middle of the street were full of weeds. The families who had built the big houses lived somewhere else now. Only old people lived in them, or a few young people who were poor.

The boys in the college building were all asleep this early

in the morning. Later in the day they would emerge and their voices would rebound strangely on the quiet air, like an echo from glass, Mr. Eliot thought. They were all nice trim boys, but Mr. Eliot could never tell one from another. His wife used to pay them to clean up the yard, and sometimes she would make one come in the house and talk to her. Mr. Eliot didn't take an interest in them. He and his wife were different kinds and she had had the habit of talking when there was nothing to say, but they had got along all right. Mr. Eliot pecked on the windowpane with his fingernail, which was overgrown and pointed like a bird's claw, and left the room. He crossed quickly to the other side of the house, where there was a window he liked better.

This room was piled waist-high with old books and ledgers. Mr. Eliot could have told anyone who wanted to know exactly what was in the room and how to get to it, though the piles would have looked hopelessly confused to a stranger. He didn't look at the books now, however. There was a path from the door to a window on the other side of the room, and he had put a chair by the window. There was an old pair of field glasses on the sill.

The window overlooked a net of alleys behind the row of houses where Mr. Eliot lived. In the early morning the people in the houses got up and let their dogs out on the alley and went back to sleep for an hour. For that hour the world belonged to the dogs. They had leaders and wars and intrigues, carousing through the broken-down sheds and abandoned shrubbery in the alleys. Ruined objects dumped back there were full of interest for the dogs. Mr. Eliot could see it all from his window, and he followed the most interesting events with the field glasses. The dogs were never bored and he wasn't either while he was watching them. When the dogs had all been called back to their houses he knew he had better get dressed and go downstairs and eat something.

His house was a gigantic gray stone structure, and he had long stopped trying to keep it clean. It was divided in his mind into friendly and hostile zones. Upstairs every area was hostile except the bedroom and the window over the alley. The other two rooms were so full of accumulated rubble that it was hazardous even to open their doors. All the stuff was packed and organized, though; he didn't like to throw things away. The fourth door on the hall upstairs led to a balcony, where it wasn't safe to walk.

These rooms made three sides of a rectangle around the stair rail. The space between the rail and the rooms was empty, except for a soiled Indian rug and a roll-top desk with the roller broken. The desk was jammed with small clutter, like the rooms, but Mr. Eliot had to use some of the things in the desk occasionally. The stairs made three right-angle turns around a vacant space in the center and descended into the ground level. They were dark, dirty and grand, and smelled of musty stone. The stairs were a hostile zone, much too wide and long for Mr. Eliot, who was a small man. Also, like the other hostile zones, the stairs were very dimly lit. Mr. Eliot went down them very slowly for fear of killing himself with a fall. He had hung a basket from the big banister down the stairwell on a long rope, to save his having to carry things up and down, and the basket swayed lightly while he was on the stairs.

The living room was at the foot of the stairs, a large hostile area. It was a showplace for the antique furniture that had belonged to his wife and for the venerable dust on it. Mr. Eliot never sat on any of the stuff himself, but he knew if he got rid of it the place would look like an empty warehouse. He had made a safe spot up against one wall, with a sofa, a chair, two strong lamps, and the television set. When the good shows came on at night Mr. Eliot would sit there with a blanket around him, and things would be fine. The only problem was moving from point to point in the house, outside the light, in the enormous shadows.

In the morning this room was merely dim. The ceilings and windows were high and the light that filtered through the panes was stained. Near the front door was a heavy upright piano with a broken flute on top of it. On the piano was an oval mark in the dust where Mr. Eliot's fiddle had stayed before he carried it off to the kitchen. Mr. Eliot stood looking into this room with distaste until he was rested enough from the stairs to go get his breakfast.

The kitchen was the smallest room in the house and the kindest. It was painted clear green and was well lit by a large bare bulb hanging from the ceiling, and there was no secret dirt in it anywhere. There was a table with an enamel top and a chair where Mr. Eliot sat down to eat his shredded wheat. The kitchen door opened onto the back yard, the alley side of the house, and he left it open today so he could smell the spring coming. When he had eaten he washed the bowl and dried it and put it up, and he put up the box and the bottle of milk. The coffee was heating on the stove. Mr. Eliot went out the kitchen door and walked around the house to pick up his paper from the front porch.

He spent a long time with the paper, sitting in the kitchen with the door open. When he was done he had read everything in it. That way it helped fill up the morning, and Mr. Eliot would not watch soap operas and game shows on TV the way some old people did. That thought arrived along with a little pain in his back, and he got up and stood in the doorway, looking at the wire pen where he used to keep bird dogs. He had liked having them there, but he didn't think it was fair to a dog like that to keep him penned up and never hunt. He quit thinking about dogs and went to sit down on the chair again. It was this time of day, when he was through with the paper and there was nothing to watch on television for hours, that bothered him.

At five o'clock there was always a movie, and when it was over it would be time to fix supper. The sun would be going down while he cooked, making a pretty light in the room. He would drink some whiskey before he ate. When he had cleaned up he would have another drink and watch more television. Some nights he played his fiddle instead.

The case would go on the table with the bottle and glass, and he would take the fiddle out. His bow had lost all the hair out of it, so he now played with a broken yardstick. Where it touched the strings it was dark and shiny and the advertising had worn away. He played everything he knew while the dark came into the kitchen and deepened there. In the dark his hand found notes or the glass along with his thought instead of just after. As he got near the bottom of the bottle he played things he had never known, moving in a heavy, certain suspension full of sound, a shadowy fluid.

In the end the fluid would enter every room of the house, washing the dimness away. Mr. Eliot moved freely then, not from light to dark boundaries but in the common absorbing night of the world. An electric power animated him and he felt little bonding to the body he carried with him. It was a pitiful stranger, but he was compassionate toward it. Secure in the flowing darkness, he guided the strange body up the stairs, carefully and patiently put it to bed. If the morning was cloudy the body could sleep longer, but Mr. Eliot never drew the shade.

That was what his days were like and now when he thought of it he felt like he was about to be sad. He leaned forward in the chair, dragging his fingers across the pitted enamel table top, trying not to think. He looked at the drawer under the table and remembered something. There was a gun in there, a tiny .22 rifle that broke down in sections. It wasn't a good gun; all the good ones were packed away upstairs. Mr. Eliot couldn't remember why he had this rifle; he had no respect for it and had thrown it in the drawer like a bread knife. Everything on it that should have been wood was plastic. Still it had a peep sight and he thought it would be light enough for him to handle. So he knew what he could do today. He would take the little rifle and shoot pigeons.

There were swarms of pigeons all along the street, and Mr. Eliot loathed them, for no real reason. They were fat and unclean. The small lurid colors on their heads and legs offended him. Often they congregated on the roof and balcony, which was really an open sleeping porch, and Mr. Eliot, who had now assembled the gun, decided he would go up there to shoot them.

The idea excited him more than anything had for a long time, and he went up the stairs rapidly, not noticing the effort in his delight. He went quickly to the desk and raked through the contents in its top, spilling out old envelopes, a cluster of dusty blue and green feathers, a dry stamping pad, and a splinter of horn. Under these things Mr. Eliot found a half-full box of .22 short cartridges. He loaded the gun and put the box into his shirt pocket.

Standing at the door Mr. Eliot felt a little quaky, but he pushed the feeling from himself. The door opened stiffly and cried a little as the hinges turned around. There was also a screen door on the outside, and the screen had rusted and was torn in places. The tips of the broken wires were still bright and they gleamed from indirect sunlight, catching Mr. Eliot's attention for a moment. Gray light illuminated the roofed porch, which smelled indistinctly of dung. Mr. Eliot saw a blurred bird turning to land on the dirty railing, and he went through the screen.

The bird stayed on the railing, walking along it obliviously. For some reason Mr. Eliot couldn't see clearly and it might have been any kind of bird. He knew it was moving but he couldn't quite tell what it was doing. He heard a clear sound and thought then that he must have fired the gun. There was a shape moving dully in one place on the rail and Mr. Eliot began to see a glowing ring around it. He wondered if he had hit the bird, and his blood jumped hard in his veins.

Mr. Eliot felt them breaking. When he was stretched on the floor his cheek felt immeasurably cool and comfortable against the old boards, and he saw himself straightening, elongating, and moving far away.

· 3 ·

For the bull the first different thing about the day was that there was no food. There was a hole over the feedbox in the stall, and every day in the morning and at night a man's hand came through it and put crushed corn in the box and lowered a bucket of water. The bull was a year old and it happened like that every day. Nothing else ever happened. The bull hadn't been out of the stall since he had been born into it. Today there wasn't any food. The bull moved restlessly over the straw on the floor, flaring his soft red nostrils. Muscles waved through his neck and back, and he hooked up some straw on his horns.

A strange man opened the door a little crack. His arms were long and covered with black hair, and he grinned with brown teeth at the bull. He showed a loop of rope to the bull, who lowered his head and blew into the straw. The man was Beasely and he knew just what he was doing. He flipped the rope and pulled it tight around the bull's horns.

Beasely opened the door wider, and the bull smelled a horse, which he had never done before, and saw open sunlight. He walked easily out of the stall. Beasely was already on the horse, snubbing the rope to the saddle horn. He and the horse both knew the game, but the bull was ignorant. He was thrilled and astounded to be loose in so much air. The morning was so foggy that the sun had become a white dim circle. The horse moved and tightened the rope so that the bull had to follow. He dropped to his knees and bellowed and refused to walk. Beasely had to drag his full weight for half a mile, which he did, laughing and swearing the whole way.

When they stumbled into the lot where the truck was waiting, the bull went berserk for a few minutes. He snapped one horn and shook the rope off. There was blood on the rope and on the bull's shiny black hide. The bull surged around the lot, doing what he pleased. He found a cedar sapling and began to slam his head at the base of it. While he was kneeling in front of the tree the sun turned red and the fog was streaked with color. After he had demolished the sapling he was tired and his head hurt. He stood still for a moment.

Beasely had quit laughing. He knew he couldn't use the horns again; he'd have to go around the neck, which would be a mess. He thought the bull might be fool enough to strangle himself, but there wasn't any other way. The bull's voice came out in an echoing gurgle when the rope sank into his neck, and he set his legs while Beasely pulled him up to the truck. He passed the rope through the grid at the back of the truck to hold the bull there. There wasn't any ramp, so Beasely had to lift the bull's front legs into the truck and hope he'd jump in. It didn't work out, and they struggled clumsily by the tailgate. Finally Beasely walked around behind the bull and tried to lift him by the hips. The first time he tried the bull fell all the way out. He rested some before he tried again, and that time the bull scrambled on up. As he went in the truck a stray leg hit Beasely in the center of the chest and he fell down on the packed ground.

The gate of the truck hung open and the bull stood quietly, up toward the cab. He was relaxed now that things seemed to be over, turning a calm liquid eye through the grille. Beasely's face turned from white to red. He coughed, started breathing, and stood up. His hands knocked dirt off his trousers and closed the gate of the truck. He turned the horse out in the lot and went to the cab.

"You rascal," he said to the bull, "what did you do that to me for?" He stood with one foot in the truck looking for his sunglasses before he started the engine. When the truck began to roll the bull lurched and adjusted his stance to the foreign motion. It felt like the world was coming apart under his feet. A plume of white dust blew up behind Beasely's wheels as he drove the bull sixty miles to the slaughterhouse at Murfreesboro, where they cut him to pieces and wrapped them in brown paper. By then the sun had burned all the mist away and turned yellow, and every single mote of dust glowed golden in the bright air before it settled to the ground.

II

◆

The Structure and Meaning
of Dormitory and Food
Services

✦

FOR FOUR OR FIVE straight days they brought the blind
kid to my table and it made me very uncomfortable. Of
course there couldn't have been any particular purpose behind it. I ate in the outermost hall, near the entrance, which
was obviously the best place to take him. There were always
people milling around through all the halls, and if they tried
to take him very far past the door he would have been sure
to create what is known as a "flow problem." But there were
lots of tables right near the door, and I didn't always sit at
the same one, so I didn't understand why they kept bringing
him to mine.

What I'm talking about is a place called Commons, where
the freshmen and sophomores of Princeton University (a
group of underprivileged beings to which I used to belong)
go to eat. From the outside it's a grandiose neo-Gothic
building whose original purpose must have differed slightly
from what it is at present. Inside it's a network of rooms and
passages that coil around and embrace one another endlessly,
after the fashion of the enormous serpent that is said to sit
coiled at the center of the earth.

The hall where I had my disconcerting encounters with
the blind kid in such rapid succession is sometimes referred

to as the main hall, not because it's the most popular but apparently just because it's the first hall you are likely to encounter if you assume the role of freshman or sophomore and enter the complex in search of food. From the path outside you go in through a pair of large paneled doors set in a rounded arch and turn to the left, following the person or persons ahead of you. Before you have gone very far, you meet a functionary behind a desk. He probably has on a green coat, and he will require you to produce either a meal card or a certain amount of cash. Once you have satisfied him, you are free to enter the serving line. If you get confused, just keep following the people ahead of you and do whatever they do. Get a tray and silverware and proceed to the steam tables, which are equipped with runners for your tray to slide on. Through a glass partition you see pans of steaming food, and behind the pans some people are standing around with ladles. They have on paper hats and paper aprons. Food is served cafeteria style; ask these people and they'll pile a plate with as much as you want. It doesn't look very appetizing, but don't worry about that. At the end of the warming tables you can serve yourself a drink, and then you find that you are facing an open doorway. Continuing to follow the people ahead of you, go through this doorway, cross a short hall, and go through a second doorway. Now you have to stop and make decisions, but first step aside from the door so the people behind you don't knock you down. Take a deep breath. You are now in the hall from which all these apparent non sequiturs first took flight, which I might as well tell you is called Madison Hall.

The ceiling, in this hall and in all the others, is about eighty feet high. It is arched and the arches are outlined with dark wood, which produces an elegant and striking effect. The walls are punctured with long narrow lead-paned windows. In the daytime these windows admit only thin strips of light, and at night, of course, no light at all. The dimness makes this area look abandoned, and as a matter of fact it just about is abandoned; none of this gorgeous lofty space is ever used for anything. In a couple of weeks you won't notice it anymore.

The hall is longer than it is wide, and along the two long walls, about eight feet off the floor, are rows of yellow lamps which cast a dreary illumination on the rows of tables that fill up the hall. (Look at the tables right near where you're standing. You haven't got a chance of picking me out, but you might be able to find the blind kid, because I'm going to describe him to you later. But by then you might not be here anymore.) The people at these tables are not integrated with the architecture. They look like refugees camping out in a church. They are slumped over their trays, eating sullenly. There is not much conversation, and what there is is not inspiring. Most of these people want to keep on being strangers to each other, and that's why they keep their eyes fixed on their food. They aren't pretty, and they don't look happy. There's plenty of room at these tables, but if you want to have a happy and successful undergraduate career, you'd better not sit down.

Go halfway down this hall and through a small door in the left wall. You are in a long low narrow tunnel whose walls are painted yellow. People who have finished eating are coming very quickly in the opposite direction, and they don't care if they bump into you or not, so you've got to be careful. There's a sharp turn at the far end of the tunnel, and fortunately there's a mirror hanging there, which lets you see if it's safe to turn the corner. When you've gone around the corner you're in another hall, exactly like the first one except for its name (Upper Eagle) and its population.

Upper Eagle is really much more cheerful. Everyone is talking brightly, and the noise is deafening. The young men tend to be handsome and clean-cut, though a little tousled, naturally, since they're college students. They have on khakis and Levi's and Brooks Brothers shirts, all of which may show discreet signs of wear. On the backs of their chairs you'll find tweed or down jackets, and you may notice that some of the men are wearing horn-rimmed glasses. Their women are either pretty or think they are, which is just as good. It's a shame there're so few of them. Most of them are mannishly dressed, but there are a few skirts here and there. The ones who wear make-up try not to let it show. Everyone is flirting like crazy and seems to be having a good time.

They're a happy bunch, and they also have table manners. If you recognize this group as your natural element, and if it will receive and accept you, you are fortunate blessed. Sit down and eat what the Lord has provided. If not, read on.

There's lots lots more about Commons that the people you just met never know much about. For a start, there are two other dining halls open to the public, only you have to go outside to get to them. They are across an open-air arched passage from each other, and their names are Upper and Lower Cloister. Lower Cloister is called, in the meaningless jargon of the powers that be, a "health food facility," suggesting that it serves yogurt and dried fruit and doesn't serve beef, though it does serve chicken occasionally. After you go through the door you go down a flight of stairs to get to this hall, which puts it a floor below the other three. Upper Cloister isn't any different from Madison Hall. It's even connected to it, but the connecting door is usually locked.

All these four halls are inside one great sprawling building and they are linked together by an insane rabbit's warren of kitchens. The general dining public isn't allowed in these kitchens, but many students do get to go in there, because all the menial and low management jobs are held by students. I got to know some workers and I was taken into the kitchens, but first things first.

When I first came to Princeton I lived in two rooms with two other students. The building we lived in, Lockhart by name, adjoined a street that defines the western edge of the campus. Right on the corner is Commons.

On the fall afternoon when we arrived, the two other students and I selected one iron frame bed each and made it up. We packed our clothes into identical dressers. We indulged in a little strained conversation until it was dinnertime. Then we put on our coats and walked up to Commons. One of my roommates had on a gray tweed coat, and the other was wearing a down jacket, although it was a warm evening. They went straight to Upper Eagle. God knows how they knew.

Once we had sat down in Commons we could talk about the food. They both agreed that it wasn't too bad. Both of them had gone to prep schools where the culture was as high as the tuition and the food was truly vile. Commons was an improvement as far as they were concerned. I didn't think it was bad myself, for institutional food. There were three kinds of salad dressing that I liked and I didn't get tired of them for several months.

For a couple of months I was a fine student who made a smooth adjustment to college life. I went to all my classes, even to the ones at nine o'clock, and took busy little notes once I got there. The classroom buildings were all at the opposite end of the campus from our dormitory and there were lots of other dormitories in between. Most of these buildings are nice neo-Gothic buildings, sufficiently impressive if you're not so snobbish as to compare them unfavorably with their models. Some of them are administration buildings, with names like Nassau Hall and West College. There is a classroom building called McCosh and one called East Pyne, and other ones as well. There is a large chapel and an enormous library. I won't go into all the names of dormitories. These buildings are all hooked up in a vast mesh of flagstone paths. The master path of all the paths is called McCosh Walk, and that's the one we used to get from our dorm to our classes. The others don't have names.

So every day I went to classes and admired the architecture and smiled at the people I would meet on the paths, and every evening I went to Commons for dinner and strained conversation with my roommates. At night I went to the library and worked on my homework until it was bedtime. There was a lot of studying to do, but I won't dwell on that. The structure and meaning of Firestone Library is an entirely different subject.

Winter came and it snowed all over the place. Students walking on the paths packed the snow into a single impenetrable glassy sheet of ice, which was excruciatingly difficult to walk on. It was less fun to go to classes under these conditions. Moreover, I developed insomnia. I lay awake at night and if my roommates snored it bothered me and if they didn't the silence got on my nerves. I used to hear sounds of faraway applause, diminishing and returning over and over, and although I knew it had to be the steam heat I couldn't convince myself that that was all; I thought I was losing my mind. After this sort of bad night it was hell to go to a nine o'clock class, but I kept going. For a while.

I never got terribly adept at going through the tunnel between Madison Hall and Upper Eagle. People ran into me a lot, and I used to get food on myself. One night the mirror got knocked out of phase and it pointed straight at me as I hurried after my roommates, trying not to dump my tray. In the mirror I looked sad and desperate. My hair was long and greasy, and there were black rings around my eyes. My shirt-tail was out and I had food spills on my shirt. Not all of them were fresh, either. Obviously I was headed in the wrong direction.

After that night I started eating in Madison Hall with

other people who looked more or less like me: bicycle buffs, science fiction nuts, opera fans, owners of elaborate calculators, Class A chess players, and the like. These people don't talk while they eat, so I had an opportunity to pay more attention to my food, only I was fairly disenchanted with the food by then. The salad dressings no longer charmed me, and the vegetable dishes began to seem too hazardous, so I ate mostly dead meat, corn, and potatoes. It didn't help either my digestion or my humor.

There was one excellent vegetable that I do remember from that period, standing in muscular contrast to all the rest. In midwinter Commons miraculously acquired a huge supply of fresh broccoli, and I learned to love it. For over a month they served it almost every other day, and I always ate a couple of large knots of the stuff. It brightened up my life no end.

One day I went in to lunch and saw that they had marinated a lot of this broccoli and put it out on the cold table. The sight pleased me for two reasons: first, I am very partial to marinated things; second, the cold table is self-service, so that I wouldn't have to be ashamed of my greed. I took a full plate of nothing but broccoli and scampered over to the nearest table. When I bent over my tray, drops of blood fell on it; my nose was bleeding. I dabbed it a little with a paper napkin, and placed a stalk of broccoli in my mouth. It was succulent and delicious. A thin stream of blood ran down my upper lip. I trapped it in my napkin and leaned far back, the napkin pressed to my nose. I rolled my eyes around to see if anyone had noticed, but no one was looking at me; the people beside me and across from me were all champing along blindly, completely self-absorbed. I let a few moments pass, lowered my head, and took another piece of broccoli. My mouth filled with blood, which I swallowed, and again I tipped my head back.

The obvious correct action was to leave Commons, go

back to my room, and lie on my back until my nose stopped bleeding. I considered this possibility for a bit, but I couldn't bear to give up the broccoli. My blood had run back to wherever it came from, and as long as I kept my head back it seemed likely to stay there. Cautiously, I found my plate with my fingers, and began to pump broccoli into my mouth by touch. This operation must have looked very peculiar, but either no one saw or no one cared. With my head back I couldn't see anyone around me. My gaze was fixed on the beautiful airy ceiling. Outside the windows the wind was snapping the tree branches around, and there were moving gray clouds, packed with future snow. All this was a much more pleasant visual prospect than the inside of Madison Hall, and it made me feel content. By the time I mopped up all the broccoli, my nose had stopped bleeding.

This incident, which I thought had passed unobserved, ended by netting me a new roommate. He was a Commons worker, and he ate in Madison Hall, where most of the workers eat when they're working. He was also a Class A chess player, which has nothing to do with anything. I won't re-create the embarrassing conversation we had about the broccoli; the important point is that his roommate wanted to swap and so did I, and so we did. For his roommate the move to my room was the first step of a long and tortuous social climb that ended . . . ah, forget it.

I moved into a single small room, same building as previously, with identical beds, dressers, and desks, two each. My roommate's name was Victor Immermann, and he was a German Jew, actually a second-generation immigrant. He didn't have any Jewish habits that I could recognize, except that in our window he kept a thing with candles in it which I forget the name of. This object had been a cruel embarrassment to his ex-roommate, but I didn't care about it. I didn't care about anything, including becoming better acquainted with Victor. I had carried my eating habits over into my personal life, meaning that I spoke to no one if I could avoid it, and I spent most of each day sulking on my dirty sheets. I had quit going to a lot of my classes, and I didn't study at the big library anymore. If Victor was around I barely noticed him, and I avoided him at meals.

Victor did have one thing that interested me: a key, or a copy of a key, which he had swiped from a student manager. If you wanted it to, this key would let you into Commons late at night when everyone was gone, and one night it let me and Victor in. Every light in the place was behind numerous shadowy objects and seemed to be located a few inches off the floor. There was plenty of noise, even though there was nobody there. All through the kitchens the machines were humming to each other, each singing its own little functional song. Victor was hopping around from one to another, in some obscene variant of disco dancing, explaining to me the names and purposes of them all. I'm sorry to say that most of his lecture didn't stick, so I can't repeat it. I just got a powerful impression of a thousand vats and cauldrons, magical slicers and peelers, miles of tubing leading who knows where, and more that I can't name, all of it shining, chromed, and mystical.

There are three floors of kitchens through which the machines burble interminably in the half dark. Above the kitchens are the offices of the professional administrators, and behind their doors the mysteries and rituals of a full-fledged corporation are performed. On a higher story yet Commons betroths itself to the Housing Office, and Dormitory and Food Services (DFS) is born. It must look neat on paper. Above all of this there is a high tower, the Commons tower, which even Victor's key can't open.

Beneath the kitchens is a web of steam tunnels, which carry heat all over the campus. Victor could have gotten us into that, but we didn't want to go, because the heat is too extreme for a person with clothes on to bear. It wouldn't be very comfortable even for a naked person, but Victor told me that sometimes naked persons would enter the steam tunnels and crawl all over campus, underneath the ground. There are grilles in McCosh Walk where these naked persons may stop for fresh air and a look at the upper world, if they like.

The steam tunnels were the lowest level that Victor's insinuating curiosity had pried into, but later I found out about at least one deeper layer. I passed by Commons late one night and saw two naked persons I knew slightly, sluicing each other off with water from a hosepipe. They had found their way under the steam tunnels somehow, into older smaller tunnels where they slithered around in mud, the same mud they were washing off when I spoke to them. They said they could have gone down lower, but they got afraid.

Victor and I left Commons through Madison Hall, and as we walked between the dark lines of tables, a number of small shadows swooped down at us from the ceiling, out of that big space which nobody uses. They were bats, and apparently they lived there. I asked Victor where they went in the daytime, and he held up his empty hands in the gesture of a man with no money and no information.

I didn't get to know Victor very much better from this excursion, but I did catch the curiosity bug. Sometimes I'd borrow his key and go prowl around Commons at night, but mostly my curiosity worked itself out in terms of towers. Although I never mastered the Commons tower there were plenty of others, with locks that were bypassable in one way or another. I accumulated a collection of crude shims and picks, and I carried a screwdriver for removing the panels of doors when necessary. My favorite towers were in Henry Hall, on the west side of campus, and in Patton, over toward the center.

From one of these towers I could look down and see all

the buildings and paths like lines on a map. I could watch people walking around on the paths as well, and speculate about what they might be up to. Sometimes my former roommates would appear down there, and I could figure out quite a bit about developments in their lives by the people they walked with and places they went. It was really loads of fun, albeit in an abstract sort of way.

One day I climbed down from a tower and discovered that Victor had burned out, cracked up, and left. And I always thought he was happy. He went off to Germany, as I later learned. You may surmise that I didn't miss him dreadfully, though his key went with him.

It was late afternoon when I found out that Victor was gone for good. I broke down his bedstead and carried it down to the storage area in the basement. After a few minutes of consideration I did the same thing with my own. Then I took the two thin DFS-issue mattresses and put them on top of each other on the floor. I stuffed my dirty linen into my desk drawers and lay down on the mattresses to look out the window.

The window opened onto an alley that ran from the courtyard to the street. About ten feet away from it was the brick wall of another building; superficially it wasn't much of a view. The acoustics of the alley simultaneously cushioned and amplified the noise of the cars that swished up and down the street, thus creating a very soothing and restful sound for me to listen to. And the opposite wall was really lovely in its own way. Its bricks were all the different brick colors, and some of them were blue, and they altered their shades as the time of day changed. I could have watched them forever, and in fact I almost did.

The two buildings were positioned in such a way that a very slim shaft of sunlight came in the window and struck the opposite wall. It was no wider than a pencil, and it spanned the wall from floor to ceiling. As a day went by this line of light would crawl along the wall from the window to the door. I often thought that if I made marks on the wall along its path I would be able to know what time it was, but this scheme, like most of the ones I evolved while lying on my mattresses, never got translated into action.

Over in West College, a whole big building full of nothing but secretaries and provosts, things having to do with me were happening on paper. Provosts made decisions and secretaries typed them up; cards were filed and letters were mailed out. After that shaft of light had crawled around the room a certain number of times, I wasn't a student anymore. Mother and Father could stop paying the bills. Only somehow the cards and letters never made it over to Dormitory and Food Services, and I didn't get kicked out of my room, and I could still eat at Commons. All of a sudden going to Commons was the only thing left on my schedule.

At Commons they started to bring the blind kid to my table and it upset me. The blind kid wasn't a proper member of the Madison Hall group; he was successful and well adjusted. He was a brilliant student of higher mathematics, and he played the cello wonderfully. His name was David Lehnsen. He could find his way around campus perfectly well, using a long aluminum pole to strike the ground and orient himself. The pole had little pits in it, a rubber tip, and some bright swatches of electrical tape wound around it in places. Lehnsen walked faster than a person with sight, tapping his stick rapidly, following the paths of his memory. But Commons was too confusing for him to navigate alone. When he came into the hall he would leave his pole in the vestibule and take the arm of a Commons worker who guided him through the serving line. When his tray was ready the Commons worker would carry it for him, lead him into Madison Hall and seat him safely at my table. Lehnsen and the Commons worker would exchange a few compliments before the worker went back to the line.

Lehnsen's hair was short and dark, and his face was a soft oval. He wore striped shirts and double-knit pants, as a rule. The appearance of his eyes was not abnormal, except that they never looked at anything. Lehnsen's hands floated confidently over his tray, locating all the objects on it. His thumb dipped surreptitiously over the rim of a glass to see how full it was, while a forefinger tested the edge of his plate. He ate quickly and efficiently, but sometimes some article on his tray would escape him entirely, a piece of cake or a coffee cup in a corner. I never stayed long enough to see him leave; I bolted my food and got out. After it happened a few times running, I moved to Upper Cloister.

I began to get letters from Victor Immermann, delivered to the door by the Italian janitor, who like all the janitors was a DFS employee. Like most of the janitors, this one was a descendant of a family of Italian woodworkers that some older and more courtly version of DFS had imported to Princeton several generations earlier. The DFS people wanted the Italians to come and do handsome woodwork for various university buildings, perhaps even in Commons. DFS offered high wages, but the Italians were wary. They wanted to know what would become of their children in a strange and potentially hostile land. The upshot was that DFS promised employment for their descendants for as long as they wanted it. Most of these descendants never learned English and so wound up as janitors.

One of Victor's letters described an American kid whom he had met in Vienna. The American didn't have much money, but he did have a Eurailpass. So he never spent money for a place to sleep. He taught himself to stay awake for a long time, more than seventy-two hours finally, and for that period he would amuse himself with the money he had or could hustle, wherever he happened to be. When he couldn't stay up any longer he'd get on a train and go to sleep. He would get off the train whenever he had slept enough, in some city at the other end of Europe from where he started. Then he would wander through the city until he found someone who spoke enough English to tell him where he was; in this case it was Victor. Letters like this one made me begin to think of Victor as someone I would have liked to meet, and I never could decide whether that was more sad or funny.

In early March all the Italian janitors decided it wasn't going to snow anymore and they came out and chipped the ice off the paths with curious long-handled shovels. Then it was much easier to get around. In the would-be grassy plots between the paths, persistent snow hung on till it turned gray.

I started going for long slow walks around the campus. I knew that I was going to give up and go away soon, and these walks all had a self-conscious feeling of finality to them. In late March there was spring vacation and not many people were around, which made my walks more pleasant; I could behave however I wanted to. One evening I just stopped still on a path and snorted the air for a few minutes. It was almost cold, but warm at the same time, the way it gets in spring, and the sky was part blue, part gray. I could smell things secretly growing.

On a path parallel to mine and maybe twenty yards away David Lehnsen came tapping his brisk way along. He passed into a shadow of a building and hesitated, appeared to lose confidence. Then he made the wrong decision, plunged off the path and got his pole tangled up in one of those sullen recalcitrant patches of snow. He retreated, found the path again, tapped the flagstones uncertainly. Finally he stopped moving at all.

I took a couple of steps along my adjacent path. Nails had worn through my boot heels and they made a distinct clack in the quiet air. Lehnsen called out to me.

"Where am I?" he said. I began to tell him.

"You are on a path in front of Dodd Hall," I said. "You are facing north. After you have gone forward for a short distance you will cross McCosh Walk and encounter a flight of stairs that passes between Whig Hall and Clio Hall. Once you are up these stairs you can walk around Nassau Hall and reach Nassau Street, where you can turn either right or left. If you head to the right you will eventually reach New York City and from there you can go wherever you like. If you go to the left you will run into Commons and . . ." I would have gone on to tell him everything I had ever known or supposed about Commons, but he had already thanked me and moved away out of earshot.

Lehnsen receded and diminished down his path, and when he got small enough I superimposed onto him my mental image of the American kid with his Eurailpass, stumbling half awake into an unknown foreign city with his eyes all gummed up and crusty with sleep. Whenever he wakes up he wakes up in the dark. Take Lehnsen and lead him through a few loops, then spin him around a time or two and he won't know where he is. And he can't find out, being blind, till someone comes along to tell him. Look at Lehnsen over there where you've left him all confused. Is he angry? Is he frightened? Will he ask you why you crossed him up? Will he ask you to straighten him out again? What will he do? What can he do? I can't answer any of these questions for you. Grope your own way through it if you want to know.

Irene

◆

IRENE — actually it's always impossible to come directly to the point. By that I mean that I will certainly have to go over some of my own monotonous history before I will be able to say anything sensible about Irene. If then. But perhaps this isn't altogether a bad thing, if you think about points, if you think about the point of a pencil for instance, you must realize that a view of at least some of the pencil is required for you to make any sense out of the pencil's point. I mean that it is even impossible to conceive of the point of a pencil without a pencil which leads up to it. Unless you consider that the mark of a pencil point on paper or some other surface is the point itself, in which case one may say that the point is perceived in detachment from its own development, yet in refutation one may also say that the pencil's point continues to exist after the mark has been made, so that to identify the mark with the point itself is clearly fallacious. But this business about marks and points and pencils is going nowhere. It tells you nothing about Irene at all, and it doesn't tell you much about me either, although the perspicacious may suspect that I have spent some time somewhere in my career reading the works of certain philosophers who go to great lengths to prove absurd things in ridiculous ways. And this, in fact, is true.

At a certain point in my life I lived for a couple of months in Newark. What I was doing before that is probably more of the pencil than anyone is interested in looking at. But I used to pass by or through Newark occasionally, before I lived there, when I traveled the trains or the New Jersey Turnpike. The prospect from the New Jersey Turnpike (between New York and Franklin Park) is truly incredible. You can't believe what the hand of man has wrought. The land would be flat if there were any land, but since you can't see any land there is no firm reason to suppose that there is any. On either side of the highway and reaching to the farthest parameter of your vision is a very complicated jungle of machinery. I have never had any idea what most of it is for. Some of it, I believe, has to do with oil refineries, and there are always plenty of busy smokestacks and mysterious little aureoles of flame. To drive through this area in the daytime is likely to be somewhat depressing. Around sunset it has a weird beauty; the horizon is penetrated by strange and inexplicable structures which organize the colors of evening according to their own unknown system, so that the spectator may feel that he has passed into some majestic created world quite alien to his own. At night this journey is a tour of hell: the smoke, the steam, the lights and flames, and nothing remotely human. You would never suspect that anyone lived there. However, many people do.

One morning I woke up with a strong feeling that it was time for some sort of radical change. Without packing a bag or notifying anyone of my decision, I went to the train station and got into a train. It was not necessary to buy a ticket, because I had a commuter's pass, and the conductor was not surprised when I fell asleep in the seat, because that was a habit of mine, too. An unusually rough stop awakened me and I left the train and began to go along the street opposite the station, looking at all the FOR RENT signs. I had brought my checkbook along, so that when I had found a suitable apartment I was able to make a payment immediately. But to sign the lease I had to leave what was soon to be my neighborhood and go to the office of a rental agent. After I had negotiated the contract and written the check, I asked the agent, quite casually, what city I was in. In this way I found myself living in Newark. I stayed in the unfurnished apartment for a night in order to familiarize myself with it, and the next day I returned to my former residence to take away my possessions.

Actually this story of how I came to Newark is as false as it is improbable. This is what really happened: One day I felt strongly that I had to make some definite alteration in my circumstances. I was at a loss to determine exactly what I should do. So I decided to resort to a familiar method of divination: selecting a book, dropping it open onto a table, and following whatever suggestions seem to be made by the passage which hazard thus chooses. The book I used for this purpose was *The Conference of the Birds* by Farid ud-din Attar, a book which I had acquired only the day before. I balanced the book on its spine and let it drop. Naturally, as the book was new, it fell shut. Slightly annoyed, I opened the book at random and began to read. This is what I read:

He who wishes to live in peace must go to the ruins, as the madmen do.

Immediately I thought of Newark. I went there on the train (I had recently sold my car) and looked in the neighborhood of the train station until I found a very cheap apartment. I stayed there for one night, and then went back to collect the various items I had accumulated in the years of my life up to then. These were mostly books and records; more practical things I had to buy.

At the outset, the radical change seemed to be working out very well, or at any rate none of the things that had troubled me before the change troubled me any longer. I went out and bought myself a set of pots and pans and for at least ten days I made myself perfectly happy by learning to cook a few simple dishes. I had never cooked for myself before (the insightful may infer that there were mothers and girlfriends in my past, and maybe institutions too) and this occupation proved to be very absorbing. Also, during the first few days of my sojourn in Newark, I was house-proud. The apartment was quite ordinary, but it did have one peculiarity. It was on the second floor and you entered it, after climbing a grimy flight of stairs, through the kitchen. The rest of the apartment was nothing more than a long rectangular room with a high ceiling, cream-colored walls with cracked paint, and four sash windows facing the street. The peculiarity was in this room, divided into a suggestion of two rooms by two wooden columns that went all the way down to the floor and all the way up to the ceiling. The columns had carved Corinthian capitals. They were stained brown. The columns had no function whatsoever, yet they pleased me enormously. At times I was even vain about them.

I conducted my life, cooking and eating and so on, on the near side of the columns, next to the kitchen. All my furniture was in this part of the room. Actually I owned no furniture, but the previous tenant had conveniently abandoned a table, a chair, two dressers in pretty bad condition, and an enormous flat-topped trunk which sat underneath the window opposite the kitchen door. The trunk was full of something; the rental agent had told me that someone would come to claim it soon. I never looked to see what was inside it, though no one ever came.

Past the columns the room was empty and always seemed spacious, sometimes grand. I did allow myself to sleep on the far side of the columns. I slept on a foam mat which I had formerly used for camping trips. I was fortunate to still have the mat; I had remembered it at the last moment, the day that I sold my car. Just before I handed over the keys it occurred to me to look in the trunk, where I found the mat and a few other items which I had left there. I rolled the mat up and went away with it under my arm; it made a compact bundle. In Newark I spread the mat out each night to sleep on, and in the morning I rolled it up and removed it, thus preserving the sacred vacancy of the space behind the columns.

In general I was very neat and tidy about the apartment, washing each dish as soon as I had used it, and so on. It was impossible to keep the apartment strictly clean, because it was summer and the windows had to be open. A strange sort of black silt used to float in through the windows and coat every available surface. Newark is part of a much larger region which is popularly known as Cancer Valley. Nevertheless, I was neat. During the first couple of days I was there I went through all my papers and threw away everything that I no longer needed and organized everything that I decided to save. I put my books into a bookcase; I put my records in alphabetical order. Without trespassing into the area behind the columns, I arranged everything so that the inhabited area, which was not large, did not seem crowded. Later I would stand in the middle of the room, or sometimes behind the columns, and admire the success of my management. Then I would cook and wash the dishes and sweep the floor. I behaved exactly as though I were expecting someone and making the place ready to receive that person. The truth was that no one was expected. I had been injured in my affections, not once but several times, and in a fit of pique I had decided to run away from my friends, and no one was coming over.

I wasn't much distressed by this enforced isolation; on the contrary, I believed that it was a very good thing. I had many foolish beliefs at that time, one of which was that loneliness and emotional pain and suffering and so forth are likely to provoke great outbursts of creative genius. I thought that one day soon I would cross over into the space behind the columns and write a book that would amaze the world, compose music that would make the world weep, invent a complete and perfect philosophy that would make the world comprehensible to itself. I intended to learn several languages and how to play the saxophone (in spite of the fact that I did not possess a saxophone). I would go into the empty half of the apartment and pace energetically for hours, entranced in a fantasy of my own glory. Otherwise I did nothing.

Delusions of grandeur prevented me from settling down to do anything. Somehow I was unable to select a book from my orderly bookshelf. Cooking and eating began to bore me (though I couldn't afford to give it up), and I decided that I had cabin fever. Then I began going for walks.

The door at the bottom of the dark staircase had once had glass panes in it, in the happier days of the neighborhood. When I lived behind it the glass was all gone, and a sheet of plywood had been tacked over the outside of the door to make it secure. Someone had cut a vertical slot through the plywood so that mail could be dropped inside. Outside, the sidewalk was covered with broken glass. There was other trash too, sometimes, but the broken glass was the main thing. The outside of the plywood on the door was coated with green paint, which tended to come off on your hand if the weather was humid. The door was loose in the doorjamb, so that I would have to push it back and forth to make the lock line up so I could turn it. Then I would go away down the street.

The population of the area was exclusively Puerto Rican, except for me. It wouldn't have been entirely unfair to call the place a slum. The rental agent had referred to it cautiously as a "nice family neighborhood," a complete waste of his powers of deception, as I had just come from the place. It was in fact a family neighborhood, though the families were poor and lived in crowded tenements, and it was reasonably safe.

On my walks I would go far away from my own block, up and down and across, memorizing the names of streets. It made me feel as though I had accomplished something when intersections became familiar, when I could go away for a good distance and return without getting lost. I would stare at people and places as if I had never seen anything like them before, which I hadn't. The streets were always full of people who didn't seem to have anything to do but jabber interminably in Spanish and throw bottles at the walls. There were little children all over the place, running, falling down, screaming, getting up again. The women seemed busier, and I would see them in the windows more often than in the street. Young girls I almost never saw. Any sort of courtship would have been too dangerous to consider even for a moment, but it still would have been nice to see a girl occasionally. But soon I began to think about the people less; I couldn't understand the language and the things I saw them doing were very much the same.

Objects held my attention for a little longer. On one street was a store that had a Doberman running loose on the roof, an amazing sight that I could never figure out. Late at night the glass would glitter on the street like something you might dream about. Slanting sunlight at evening or morning would catch a row of tenements and draw my mind an incalculable distance toward them; the same was true of certain glimpses into doorways. There turned out to be a lot of colors in a crumbling wall. The sentence I had read in Attar was vitalized by these impressions. However, it wasn't peace that I was getting from the ruins, but a kind of novel excitement which aroused indefinite expectations and eventually, of course, disappointed them. There came a day when nothing that I saw seemed new, and then the walks became less frequent. It's theoretically true that boredom comes from a dulling of your own perceptions and not from any diminution of the world outside. But boredom is boring nonetheless.

After walking had lost its appeal I devoted a great deal of my time to sitting on top of the trunk by the window. I conducted arguments against an imaginary accuser, justifying my joblessness and general inertia, claiming that in fact I was absorbing the environment and that my unconscious must certainly be very active even though my consciousness was not. Thus I retained a sense of some virtue, in spite of the fact that one of my legs got damaged from being continually pinned under my body on the trunk, so that when I did walk now, I limped. Sometimes I was convinced by the arguments I devised in my own favor, and at other times I suspected that I really was doing nothing but staring out the window.

The view became so familiar to me that even now when I wake up in the dark without knowing where I am it will sometimes imprint itself on the ceiling. There is a tall tenement building across the street which reaches to the corner on the left. From a normal sitting position on the trunk I can't see the top of it. I see that the first story is painted an unidentifiable pale color, while the upper stories are the natural shades of smoke-stained brick. At the corner there is a large sign in red letters on a white ground. The sign says JOYERÍA RAMÍREZ. Beneath it there is a grille which protects a plate glass store window. This grille is always locked because the store has shut down. To the right are two billboards. One of these has a blown-up photograph of two packs of cigarettes. The surgeon general's cautionary statement is plainly legible on the sides of them. Under the packs (but still on the billboard) is a painting representing neon tubes which in turn represent a lighted cigarette. The painted neon smoke from this cigarette is green; it travels neatly around the border of the billboard and finishes by writing the words *Salem Lights*. The other billboard is half taken up by a photograph of a Hispanic family: Poppa, Mama, Little Girl, and someone who might be Grandma. These people are very well dressed and all of them are smiling widely and innocently, and though the photograph is tightly composed they seem to be standing on the steps of a suburban home. On the right side of this billboard is this sentence, in white letters on an olive background: "*Alcanzalos con tu carino*." Beneath the sentence is a little white bell in a little white mandala, the imprimatur of the telephone company. I don't know what the sentence means, but I infer that its essential message is this: "Spend money on telephone calls." Past this billboard is a blank area on the wall which someone has tried to fill in with spray-painted slogans, but the letters are very indistinct; I think they have been painted over and have bled back through the paint. Then there are the concrete steps leading up to the doorway of the tenement; I can glimpse the beginning of a stair rail there when the light is right, and then the dirty frame of my own window. None of these things ever changed, and now they will never change for me. What did change were the cars parked along the street, the presences of people on the sidewalk, the appearances of faces in the upper-story windows.

It seems that the attention is selective even when it has no reason to be, and I found that I looked at one window, a second-story window, more than at others. In this window I could often see a fat and cheerful-looking woman, who would come and lean her elbows on the sill, spit onto the sidewalk, and stay there for a while, looking up and down the street. She was disposed to be friendly, and if she happened to notice me sitting in my opposite window she would smile and wave and shout something in Spanish, laughing when I clearly didn't understand. Sometimes a man would appear beside her in the window, a stocky little man with a mustache who I finally decided had to be her husband, although he looked a lot younger than she did. In the street below the windows there were always many little children, traveling back and forth from the door to the fire hydrant that splashed on the corner. Then there were seven or eight young men and boys drifting up and down the block, grouping together and separating. They spoke and shouted, it seemed to me, for the pure pleasure of sound, and if a drunk came down the street they would sometimes sing to him. The cars parked in the street seemed to belong to them and sometimes they would take them apart and sometimes they would get into one of them and go away for a while, but never forever or even for long. They would return, maybe late at night, bang the car doors and stay in the street, smoking and playing the big radios and staging mock fights with each other, or they would go and post themselves at the corner like lookouts. And they always seemed just very slightly menacing. In time I learned to recognize them all. Idly, I began to speculate about their lives and so on, but of course there was no way for me to really know anything about them.

One night I came around the corner, and there was a great deal of shouting, which didn't attract my attention at all, since there was always a great deal of shouting and it never had anything to do with me. But it kept on and got louder, and I looked at the doorstep of the tenement and saw at least a dozen hands in the air, waving like little white flags. "Come over, come over," people seemed to be saying. I went over. Lots of people were gathered on the steps, all the people I had become accustomed to watching from my window. Everyone was smiling and laughing and speaking rapidly in Spanish, and for the sake of good will I began to smile and laugh too, but since I couldn't speak Spanish I didn't really know what was going on.

The short man with the mustache began to say things to

me in broken English. He pointed to one of the boys on the steps and said, "He like the way your nose look. He want to sell you his hat." Then he snatched a hat off someone's head and passed it to me. I tried it on and said the most noncommittal thing I could think of. This remark was translated and produced considerable laughter. I gave the hat back.

The short man pointed to someone else and said, "He like you very much, he say, you come live his house and you don't have to work." Everyone laughed a lot. I laughed also. Then I said something and everyone laughed some more. This sort of thing went on for a while. I sat down on the sidewalk and lowered my head, looking up occasionally to meet the glance of someone who was being indicated to me. Whenever I looked up there were so many flashing eyes and teeth that I had to look away again. I was having trouble keeping up my end of the conversation. There was a continuous incomprehensible uproar. I began to doubt the good faith of the interpreter. I began to suspect that a trick was being played on me. I began to feel embarrassed.

I stopped raising my eyes all the way to people's faces, and on one such aborted glance I caught sight of a different sort of face, between two sets of shoulders, someone on the back step, someone with fine features, very nearly beautiful, long thick black hair, bright brown eyes I met for something less than a second. Irene's eyes, it seemed to me, were glowing with intelligence and sympathy and also, I have to admit, with amusement. I had never seen her before, and the amusement seemed to belong to someone who didn't get out much and didn't have a lot of entertainment. I looked away from her immediately, though I was tempted to stare; I thought that that would get me teased in a worse way at best, and at worst provoke some more serious misunderstanding. But I thought that I wouldn't mind being a clown for Irene, if she really thought I was so funny. She wasn't like the rest of them, who prowled the street like big lazy cats all day, who were always bored with everything and would be bored with me tomorrow.

The short man had begun bringing discarded articles of clothing from a trash pile nearby, and he was trying to put them into my pockets. I knew it was time I went away. I got up and knocked the glass dust off my pants (which was very funny), and backed away across the street, bowing and smiling and waving goodbye. I worked my key in the tricky lock and went through the door and stood behind it in the dark. I could hear them still in the street, through the transom which also let in a little light, and farther down the block there was salsa music and breaking glass. Far away in another direction a siren was winding slowly up the highway. After that whenever I sat in the window I watched for Irene.

Irene was certainly no older than twelve, but she had natural poise. She also had a head of hair that any woman would have been proud of, although Irene herself probably didn't even know it was there. The hair was long, thick, heavy, lustrous, and black. Spread out, it completely covered her shoulders, but more often she kept it in a single braid behind. Irene's posture was excellent and she walked with the dignity of a quiet child. There was also a slightly awkward strangeness about her body, a suggestion of what it would later become. My looks at her face were infrequent; though she used to smile at me sometimes it was always from a distance. I'm sure she must have thought I was peculiar. But I know her face was not becoming beautiful, it was beautiful already; the face was at least ten years older than the rest of Irene.

It's easy to say that Irene's nose was straight and her chin was strong but not too much so, but it's better to leave that sort of thing out; you can't describe a beautiful face and you might as well not try. Otherwise you get bogged down in ridiculous similitudes, which only confuse the real issue. And anyway, I was usually too far away from her to pick out her features distinctly. In the window across the street I might see something like this: Irene's hair falling a surprising distance in front of the dark bricks, the not-so-childish curve of her cheek turned upward, facing an invisible window above. She'll be a heartbreaker when she grows up, I said to myself. I fell in love with her before we had ever exchanged a sentence.

Later we did exchange sentences. Irene, it seemed, spoke perfect English, albeit a little slowly. I was sitting on my doorstep one morning, drinking a cup of coffee and rubbing my eyes open. Irene's mother sent her across the street to ask me a question. Irene came over and stopped in front of me and said, "Do you think you will be leaving your apartment soon?" Apparently there was a cousin whose wife was expecting . . . I didn't know when I might be leaving the apartment, but told Irene to tell her mother that I would let her know. Irene went back, straight across, and disappeared into the doorway.

The next time I saw her I asked her a question, "Where is the cheapest place to buy a lot of eggs?" Irene went away and spoke to her mother and returned. The cheapest place to buy a lot of eggs was the bodega beside the fish market on Fourth Street. I would have been happy to prolong the conversation, but Irene took herself neatly across the street, dodging her eight brothers who were hanging around on the opposite sidewalk, and vanished.

I imagined what she'd do inside: the good child of the family, she'd be the first up in the morning, making coffee hot and sweet and sticky, demolishing dirty dishes with the efficiency of custom. She'd change the baby and dress the toddler, sending him spinning across the floor like a wind-up toy. She'd keep an eye on him to be sure he couldn't hurt himself while she went to hold the baby in the window for a moment in which she might also glance across the street at me, smile and disappear. Midmorning I'd see her going down to the store, coming back by way of the bakery — gone again, inside with the brown sacks. Later she'd dart out the door and down to the corner, retrieving some child about to stray too far. I thought of her responsibility. I pictured her reeling the clothesline in and out, making most of the dinner, doing all of the dishes. It was rare to see her late at night and then, when her brothers out on the corner were just beginning to really wake up, I'd think that Irene had lain down on her mattress and gone to sleep abruptly, dreaming dreams it wouldn't occur to her to remember at waking.

Finally I realized that I could call Irene over to my doorway and tell her to go and ask her mother if she would let her marry me. There was a conspicuous difference in our ages of course, but I thought that in a traditional and Catholic culture the idea would not be completely unthinkable. Surely Irene would be happy; she wouldn't have to move far from home. I would teach her to read and to listen to something other than salsa music. I would teach her not to spit out the window (a regrettable habit which she seemed to have formed in her less than ideal environment). New vistas would open up for Irene, and besides, I'd like the company, someone in the house to give the household rituals some point. At night I'd only hold her pigtail; I wouldn't dream of sleeping with her until she was at least sixteen. The marriage would bring me closer to the neighbors; we'd learn to tolerate each other's differences. The little tensions when our paths crossed would be gone. I let the idea linger for a while.

More days passed, and Irene got a bad haircut. Someone just chopped the front of it off short above her eyebrows, so that with her braid she looked like she was wearing a poorly constructed coonskin cap. Her appeal was not diminished, but still I didn't get around to the proposal. This idea seemed to be traveling the road of my other ideas, which apparently led into some sort of black hole. I continued to cook, eat, take walks, do nothing.

I learned to do nothing in more troublesome ways: going away to New York or Philadelphia, doing nothing there at length, spending hours on trains and buses, coming home late. During this period I noticed that Irene had taken up residence in a little corner of the vacant space in my mind. I never needed to think of her, she was just there in the corner, and if while doing nothing I noticed anything of interest I could direct some remark to her about it. The Irene-image never answered, but that was all right with me, and I always looked for her when I was home, to keep the image fresh.

I came back very late one night in the late summer, from Philadelphia I think it was — it must have been well after midnight, because there was no one on my street when I turned the corner. On second glance: Irene was in the street, alone, and that was very strange and unusual. She was standing in front of her open doorway with her hands up over her face so that I thought she must be strangling a yawn. When I got a little closer it appeared that she was crying. I squatted down in the street beside her to try to find out what was the matter. Although I tried several different phrasings, I never got the answer. Evidently in her distress Irene had lost her English. She wouldn't speak to me and she didn't want to go home either, I could see. Finally I took one of her hands away from her face and began to lead her across the street. She came along without seeming to care, with her free hand diligently rubbing her eyes, crying steadily and quietly. At the door I needed both my hands, but she just stood there waiting. When I had opened it she followed me up the stairs without having to be led. We passed through the kitchen and I turned on a lamp. Irene went straight to the only chair, sat down, put her elbows on the table, and continued to cry.

I tried to think of something good to do for Irene, but I had nothing much to say to her. I didn't know what might distract her. I had nothing in the house to tempt a child with, nothing to eat but potatoes and coffee, nothing to play with but books and records. Irene was enclosed and unreachable in her weeping. I could think of nothing to do that wouldn't be ridiculous and beside the point. I raced my imagination; what could I say to her? I didn't know any amusing stories. Irene cried on and I sat on the trunk with my back to the window, feeling enormous, clumsy and stupid. Her face was getting dirty with tears. I wondered what she might think of the place: queer dusty intellectual clutter on one side and absolutely nothing on the other. Would she wonder what I was doing with an empty room in my house? Irene had probably never even seen an empty room. What was the point of having an empty room? Irene stopped crying all by herself and raised her head. I dampened a towel and brought it to her, letting her clean her own face. Irene finished with the towel and put it down, folded. She stood up, glancing at me briefly and then away. Her eyes scanned the whole apartment in one rapid circular sweep, then went out of focus. Her timidity had apparently returned with her composure.

"Well," I said, a little crossly. "You're all right now? There's nothing that you need?" Irene nodded. She went into the kitchen and stopped at the door to look back inquiringly. "Good night," I said, as sweetly as I could. "Cheer up . . . And you can come back if you feel like it," though of course I knew she wouldn't. I listened to her feet going lightly down the stairs. Presently I saw her from my window, crossing under the cold streetlights, sober, erect, solemn, until I lost her in the shadows of her door. I had the sort of headache I might have had if I had been the one crying. I went down and locked up after Irene.

All this, of course, was long ago, and by the night when Irene was overcome by her purely private sorrows I had already cooked and eaten my way through most of the sale of my car, and I knew that finally I was going to have to do something. Shortly thereafter, one of my aimless trips to surrounding cities landed me a job of sorts. After that I moved out of Newark. On the whole, things got better for me. I got rid of my more ludicrous ambitions and applied myself to the others a little more seriously. But I know that I will never forget Irene, because she's stuck in my head at the intersection of the imagined and the real, because it's too bad I could never get to know her, because she's human in a way that I won't ever be. Irene is grown up now, I'm sure she's been married for a while, she's probably hideously fat. Her life is completely taken up with practical necessities; no doubt she's forgotten that she ever was a child, and certainly she'll never have the idleness of mind in which she might remember me. Still I hope that on occasion, walking down some street so well known it's invisible, or turning some thoroughly familiar corner, Irene will feel perplexed a little, without knowing why, and that I will be the reason.

The Lie Detector

◆

My apartment in Hoboken had a water circulation heating system. There was a boiler in a closet by the stairs, which heated the water and pumped it into pipes that ran above my ceiling, under the roof, and finally the water got dumped into the radiators in my apartment, one in the kitchen, one in the bedroom. The pipes were not insulated and the fact that they ran through the ceiling made the whole system very inefficient. The boiler ran on electricity paid for by me, and I had been warned by the previous tenants that it could kick up the utility bill as much as a hundred dollars a month. For that reason I wasn't altogether sorry when I found out that I was going to be evicted from the place, even though the base rent was very low and I knew I would never find another place quite so cheap.

Mr. Evans, the landlord, came by to see me one rainy morning, on the first of October. It took him a long time to get me to come down to the door. I was lying on my mattress looking at the ceiling and listening to the water drip on the roof, and I wasn't expecting anyone to come over. The entrance door was at the bottom of a crooked staircase that went down from the second floor to the street. The previous tenants had made a doorbell by running a string through a slot in the door up to a set of chimes that hung inside the apartment. Someone in the street could pull the string and the chimes would ring and you would know that someone wanted to see you. But I didn't really know anyone in Hoboken and the Spanish kids in the neighborhood kept pulling the string, which annoyed me, so I cut the string and the chimes were silenced. The kids would sometimes throw firecrackers through the slot too, but they could never get them very far up the stairs, so that didn't bother me so much.

Mr. Evans banged on the door for a while and finally he gave up and let himself in with the key. He came into the stairwell and started calling. I heard him and went to the head of the stairs. Mr. Evans looked more like a doctor or a professor than a slumlord, and in fact he wasn't much of a slumlord. He owned only a few buildings, and probably it had been a nicer area when he bought them. He was about sixty, a fairly tall man with salt-and-pepper hair and practical black glasses. He had a nagging cough. On this rainy day he was wearing a trench coat, but his hair was damp and his glasses had steamed. When I came to the head of the stairs he had taken his glasses off and was wiping them with his handkerchief.

Mr. Evans heard me arrive and he looked up and put his glasses back on. He had come to tell me some bad news, he said. He was so sorry, but he had sold the building, and I was going to have to move out. I nodded my head to him. There was no light in the stairwell, except for a little dirty illumination that came in over the transom. I couldn't see Mr. Evans very well, and I'm not sure if he could see me at all. But he went on being very pleasant and polite. He told me I could have the month to move, and he warned me that he would be coming with the buyer to look the place over again. Then I thanked him for coming out and doing it the nice way. We exchanged a few compliments and apologies, and Mr. Evans said goodbye and went out and shut the door.

I listened to the lock clicking shut as Mr. Evans turned his key. Then I walked back into my apartment and went to the window. I could see him walking away down the broken sidewalk in the gray rain. It was too bad to lose the place, but I thought Mr. Evans had handled it very nicely. He could have just told me in a note or a phone call, and he didn't have to give me a month's notice at all, because I wasn't holding a lease on the place. At the moment I was even touched that he had come out in the rain to talk to me, but that was before I found out that he was going to cheat me out of my security deposit.

It was cold in the apartment. I went into the kitchen and put some water on to boil. Since I didn't want to run the circulation system, I used to try to warm up the place a little by boiling water on the stove. Sometimes it seemed to help. Anyway I could steam my hands over the pot. It was unusually cold for October and that had taken me by surprise. I had been thinking about moving to some place with furnished heat by November. I had been thinking about a lot of things and not doing any of them, and I thought now that the eviction might be a blessing in disguise, because it would force me to go out and deal with people again.

For the past few months I had done practically nothing and seen practically no one. I was recuperating from a bad love affair, and I spent the summer and early fall in suspended animation, watching my brain turn itself inside out. Time went by and my mind slowly filled itself with the salsa music and the Spanish voices that came drifting out of the rows of tenements, across the streets full of broken glass, and my memory of the lost woman diffused itself into the heavy air and the concrete of sidewalks and buildings. By the time it got cold this mental rotation was more or less complete, but I had become fixed in a routine that demanded nothing from me other than that I read the *New York Post* and eat something occasionally and watch my fingernails grow. I had the habit of inertia, but Mr. Evans's visit had broken that.

On Wednesday I got up at four and went into New York, so I could be in Sheridan Square by five, when the *Voice* came out. I picked up the paper and walked down Bleecker Street through the cold morning fog and went into a twenty-four-hour Greek diner, where I bought a cup of coffee and a piece of crumb cake for breakfast. I ate the crumb cake and started reading the ads in the back of the paper. *Voice* ads are about the only way to find a place to live without paying a broker's fee, and I didn't have any extra money to give to brokers.

I was considering moving into Manhattan, but there wasn't anything that looked too promising there. I didn't want to live in the worse parts of the Lower East Side, and I didn't think I would be very popular in Harlem. But there were a few nonspecific ads, and I thought that I would call those places, just for luck. I drank my coffee and smoked my cigarette. When I paid the check I bought a couple of dollars' worth of dimes.

The sun was beginning to eat up the fog by the time I left the diner, and I appreciated that. I had on a cloth coat that wasn't too warm, but it was all I had at the moment. It was a little before seven and there was no one else around except some garbage men. The cafés and boutiques along Bleecker Street hadn't opened yet. Really it was even too early to start making business calls, so I decided to walk over to Second Avenue. It would kill time and there was a quiet Russian deli over there, with a pay phone on the wall.

By noon that day I was shaking from coffee, I had about five of my dimes left, and I knew I wasn't going to live in Manhattan. I was sitting on a concrete island in the middle of Houston Street, looking down on a flock of pigeons which were trying to work up the nerve to come peck my shoelaces. I folded the *Voice* to another page and started reading the Brooklyn ads. Then I spent some more time on the telephone.

The next day I was in Williamsburg, a Brooklyn neighborhood I had never even heard of, on the far side of the bridge at the end of Delancey Street. I went over to look at a small apartment in a small row house out there, but by the time I arrived the woman who owned the place had already rented it to some friend of hers. She was sorry I had made the trip for nothing. She would have called me if she had known my number. If I was interested I could walk around the corner to the Galería del Sol and talk to Rick, who sometimes knew of apartments.

The Galería del Sol was supposed to be an art gallery, but it wasn't on an artsy block, and there were so few pictures that the place looked more like some kind of front. Rick was very drunk, although it was still early in the morning, and since his English was blurry it took us some time to discover that we couldn't make a deal. Rick moonlighted as a loft broker, but his lofts were too expensive for me. He didn't deal in apartments, but if I wanted to I could go down to 185 Broadway and talk to Benson, the super. Rick would have the kid go with me to show me where it was.

The kid was sitting on a trash can in front of the Galería del Sol. He had a heavy black beard and a briefcase-sized radio. Rick shouted some Spanish at him and he jumped up and set the radio on his shoulder, next to his left ear. I followed him down the street. He stayed about five yards ahead of me and never looked around. When we got to the building he unlocked the outside door and pointed me toward an apartment in the back. Then he went back in the street and sat down on another trash can, which was padlocked to a light pole, like all the trash cans in Williamsburg.

. . .

Eugenio Benson was a short coffee-colored man with square even teeth and tight knots of hair on his head. He was wearing blue coveralls with paint all over them, and when I told him what I was looking for he put on a Windbreaker and led me out around the corner, where we entered the building again through another door. There was a smell of fresh plaster in the entry, and Benson began telling me how he was repairing the walls. He showed me the elevator shaft and said that he hoped the elevator would work again sometime soon, but that wasn't a job he could do himself; Lubin, the landlord, would have to hire a mechanic, and Lubin was very slow about doing that kind of thing. But anyway the empty apartment was on the second floor. So Benson took me up to the second floor, where the replastering had not yet taken place and the walls were chipped and covered with layers of spray-painted graffiti. Benson's face folded over his smile; he folded his arms over his chest and stared at the walls. I waited for him to say something, but he didn't. In the quiet I could hear voices echoing down the staircase from six floors up and a dog barking in the light well at the center of the building.

Benson remembered me, turned around, and unlocked the apartment. We went in and walked around. The place was small but airy. I tried out the sinks, flushed the toilet, turned on the shower. Everything seemed to work. The paint was bad and there were some small holes in the wallboard, but Benson said he would fix those things, and I already believed he would do what he said. There were three steam radiators: heat furnished by the landlord. The rent was something more than I had been paying across the river, but I thought I could handle it. It could have been worse.

"I like it," I told Benson.

"Good," Benson said. "Good if you move in here, I like some more American people come in here. I don't like so many Spanish people in this building. I want some of them to go out." That seemed strange to me, because Benson was clearly Spanish himself, a Dominican as I would later learn, and my surprise must have showed on my face. Benson, who liked to communicate in gestures, took me back out in the hallway.

"Look," he said, jerking a thick arm. "Over here I want to be some American people, in here a Greek maybe, over there some Spanish people, okay, a few of them, and there some people from someplace else. I don't care who is who, but let everybody be different." Light began to dawn on me and I started to laugh. Benson looked up at me and grinned and went on. "All the Spanish people in here, they get too familiar, they in and out of all the apartments tearing everything up, they making noise all night long, till you can't live. You can't live that way." Benson started down the stairs, repeating "you can't live" like a refrain. It was a habit of his, I eventually found out.

We went back around the corner and Benson took me into his apartment. He pulled a chair out from the kitchen table for me to sit down, and called something into the back of the place. His wife came into the kitchen and her eyes widened and she nodded in my direction. Then she turned around to the stove and started making espresso. She was a large untidy woman, at least three times Benson's size. She had on a limp printed cotton dress under a loose sweater, and she was pregnant. When she had loaded the coffee pot and turned on the stove she looked back at Benson and spoke to him in Spanish. Benson hung his Windbreaker over the back of a chair and sat down opposite me.

"My wife she don't speak English," he said. "But she want to say you are welcome."

Then we started to talk about the money. It was the usual deal; a month's security deposit and a month's rent up front. I visualized my bank account, and did arithmetic in my head. I thought I could swing that and perhaps have enough left over to move and buy new sponges to clean the apartment, things like that. But I was definitely going to need a job in the near future, and that was something else to start thinking about.

"Who say for you to come here?" Benson asked me. He set his hands down on either side of the glass cup his wife had placed in front of him, and I told him about the Galería del Sol.

"This man want money from everybody he send here," Benson said, frowning. "He want one month rent."

I fell right out of the good mood I had been in. I didn't have that much money and if I did I wouldn't give it to Rick. I couldn't do it.

"I can't do it," I said.

"No," Benson said. "It's too much. Too much to ask from somebody. We don't tell him you moving in here. After while he going to forget about you."

"Will it work?" I said.

"Yes," said Benson. "When you want to move in?" I had already paid for October in Hoboken so Benson and I decided I would wait till the end of the month. I would bring the money for the deposit and advance and he would hold the apartment and my rent would start in November. I started to feel better again. The coffee pot began to gurgle and Benson's wife picked it up and poured us coffee. She offered me sugar and I refused it. She giggled and said something to Benson and giggled again.

"She say you should take some sugar," Benson said. "She say you too thin and you need it."

Benson's wife went into the main room and sat down in a wooden rocker, facing the television, which was not turned on. A three-year-old girl came out of the bedroom, stumped across the floor, and climbed into her mother's lap. Benson's wife put a hand on the girl's head and went on looking at the blank screen. She pressed her slipper against the floor and began to rock. The girl wormed her head under her mother's arm and looked at me, a sharp direct glance. She looked exactly like Benson, though she was darker and had longer hair, braided in cornrows. Her stare unnerved me a bit and I looked away from her, at the rocker and then at the other furniture in the room. There was another, similar rocker and two armchairs, all apparently hand-carved from some light wood I couldn't identify. I let my eyes coast along the wall, crossing a cabinet which looked as though it had been made by the same person, and back to the surface of the table we were sitting at. I looked up at Benson, and he heard the question I hadn't asked.

"My friend make me all these things," he said. "Man I knew when I used to be living in Santo Domingo. He make me this table you see and these chairs we sitting on and the bed in my bedroom. For me, when I get married. It nice, no?"

I nodded. I thought it was very nice.

"If I stay in Santo Domingo, I think he going to make me just one thing. The chairs maybe, or the bed. But after I get married I'm going to come in America." Benson tilted his chair and looked up. There was an ugly fluorescent tube up there and the ceiling was low, but I had a feeling it was transparent to Benson.

"Few days before I get married he take me in his house and show me all these things," Benson said. "He say to me, 'I'm giving you this present so you not ever able to forget me, mon.'"

I drank some coffee and burned my mouth. It sounded like a good trick to me. Benson would remember his friend whenever he sat down or ate something or went to bed or woke up. I wondered if I would ever forget him myself. I finished my coffee and gave Benson a twenty dollar bill to help him remember the deal until I could get back with the rest of the deposit.

. . .

It was about an hour before sunset when I got out of the PATH train in Hoboken, and it wasn't too cold, so I decided to walk down by the docks for a while before I went home. I picked my way among the gates of the different shipping yards until I found a place where I could get through to the water, on a dock below the bluffs where Stevens Institute is. I walked out to the end of the pier and sat down on an old tire. There was red light on the river from the sunset, and rainbows in the water from spilled oil. When the sun had gone down some mosquitoes came out of the water and started to bite me, so I left the pier and walked around to Elysian Park, which is up on the bluff at the corner of the Institute. I sat down on a bench near the fence and looked out across the river to where the lights of the city were getting turned on. When you look at New York from a plane or the Circle Line or the New Jersey Turnpike or just some high point on the other side of the river, the city is beautiful and coherent. When you are there it is more likely to be ugly and terrifying. I sat looking at it until the lights in the park began to come on, shutting me into their own little circle of light. Then I walked home.

I got to my building, walked up the first flight of stairs, hesitated in the dark, and climbed the second flight into the total darkness under the door at the top. I felt for the padlock there and lifted it out of the hasp, and pushed on the warped door till it opened. I could see again. I was on the roof. It was night now and I could look down and see the lights of the bars and storefront restaurants streaming up First Street toward the train station. In the other direction it was much darker, because most of the buildings down there were vacant and gutted. It was a dull, overcast night and the streetlights had a foggy aura around them. No one was out on the street. I stood there for half an hour and saw one man come out of a bar on the opposite corner and go down a side street, while I looked down at the top of his head. It was cold again and I went down into my apartment and turned on a light and put some water on to boil. I picked up my battered copy of the *Voice*, opened it to the back, and started looking for a job.

For the next couple of weeks I sniffed around for work. I passed up a few jobs because I didn't want to get locked into anything if I could help it. There wasn't much around except dishwashing and security, and those jobs would still be there when I needed them, so I tried to hold out for something better. The deposit on the Brooklyn apartment cleaned out my bank account, so I had to stop eating for a while. I called up all my contacts, trying to find some kind of freelance work that might bag me a few dollars, but I didn't have any luck. I called up Mr. Evans and told him I was moving out and would he please return my security deposit. Mr. Evans congratulated me on finding an apartment and told me he would mail the check the same day.

I got a cashier's check made up for Benson and took it out to him sometime in the middle of October. Since I didn't have keys to the building yet I had to wait on the steps and hope he would come out. There were some ten-year-old kids playing on the sidewalk and after a while I asked them where Benson might be.

"Super?" one kid said. "Super go around to the store." He pointed. I went up the first side street and found Benson coming out of the bodega on the corner. I told him I had the money, and we walked back to the building together.

"Good you bring the money," Benson said. "That way I going to get the man to come down here. Only way to get him to come down is if you got some money." The man was Lubin, the landlord. He was a Hasidic Jew and he lived at the other end of the neighborhood in one of the last big Hasidic enclaves in Brooklyn. People who knew said the area reminded them of the Warsaw ghetto. Benson opened two glass doors and we went into the hallway of the building.

"I want to get him down here," Benson said, "because I got some people need new tiles in they kitchen and the man he don't want to buy for them. He sitting up in his office saying don't give no more tiles or no more paint. But he don't ever come down here. I have to live with the people. Somebody see a nice kitchen floor, then they going to want some new tiles, and why not? That not too much to ask for."

Benson looked up and down the newly plastered hall. "You see, down here where I fix it, the building is nice. But up there on the high floors, mon, this building is one big mess. Because I been away from this building for two years. I was here a long time before, but the man he don't never want to give the money for fixing, and one day I just get tired. Then I walk out and I go get a job in a factory. And Lubin, he get another guy in here, and this guy he don't do nothing. He just let the building go down."

Benson shrugged his shoulders. "So Lubin he starts calling me. Asking me to come back in the building. I say I'm not coming, but I don't like to work in the factory. Make more money than here maybe, but it too much the same thing. Every day the same. So then I tell Lubin, okay, if he give the money to fix the building and the apartments, and if he let me pick the people for renting the apartments, then I'm coming back. So we make the deal. And here I am back. Running all around this building."

Benson did a little catwalk on the hall floor, picking his feet up high and grinning at me from the side of his mouth. Then he got serious, and stared over my shoulder through the glass doors.

"It too much work right now. But when the place be fixed right, then I'm going to keep it that way. And when people come to me asking for something, then how do I tell them no, I can't do? The man sits up there and says don't give nothing, and he don't come down here, and he can say he don't have the money for the things. I can't be that way. I got to live down here, and when I say something then that thing is me. When I say *I*, then people know they can believe it. That way, when something go wrong in the building, everybody come around saying, 'What happened? What happened?' Because I tell them the truth."

Benson looked at me and I could see his eyes coming back into focus.

"Anyway," he said, "I'm going to call the man right now. Tell him I got this money and he can come on down if he want it. Because when I get him to walk in my house, he not going to say in my face he don't have money for tiles and paint. But you come with me now and I give you the key."

I went with Benson into his apartment and gave him the check. He wrote me a receipt and gave me keys to the outside doors of the building.

"I don't give you a key for the apartment now," Benson said, "because I going to put in a new lock for you. So nobody visit you when you not home." We laughed together at that.

I left Benson and went down under the el tracks to a dairy restaurant where there were some pay phones. You could hardly hear anything with the trains going by overhead but I got lucky in spite of that and landed a day of work with Greenberg-Mellon Productions. The next morning I was out at six, driving actors to a location upstate where they were shooting a commercial for some new product that was supposed to clean mildew off boats and beach umbrellas. It was a long boring day but I got forty-five dollars at the end of it. I went to Chinatown after I dumped the van and had Three-Kinds Lo Mein and jasmine tea in a restaurant. I bought a case of noodles and some duck sauce to eat for the next two weeks and put the rest of the cash in the night depository, so I could rent a car to move my mattress to Brooklyn.

· · ·

By the last week of October, I still didn't have a job or a check from Evans. I had eaten almost all the noodles already, and I was starting to look very hard at the money I had saved to rent the car. All this was making me nervous, and I went out to see Benson to make sure everything was still okay. Everything wasn't.

"I got some bad news for you," Benson said. I finally found him in the stairwell at the east end of the building. He was putting a new pane in the window on the landing. "We got a little problem."

"Tell me about it," I said. Benson put down his putty knife and turned around, propping his elbows on the windowsill.

"Lubin took a deposit from some people," he said. "On the apartment you going to live in."

"No, I don't want to hear it," I said. "Don't tell me. What happened?" Benson pushed himself off the windowsill and turned around facing the wall.

"He took it before I had the money from you," he said. "The people went up to him and handed him the money and I didn't know. I told him not to do this. I told him I was going to find the people for the apartments, and if it can't be that way then I'm leaving like before." Benson put his fingers on the wall.

"I tell him not to and he do it anyway," he said, "so me and Lubin, we had a fight. Because I don't want these people in here. It is people taking welfare, and I don't want them, because sooner or later I know I have some trouble with them. So you going to get the apartment."

"So what is the problem," I said. Benson turned back to the window.

"What it is," Benson said. "The man don't want to give these people back they money. And somebody got to give it to them."

"Lubin's got to give it to them," I said. "He's got one deposit. From me."

"Yes," Benson said. "I tell him that and he tell me I'm holding the apartment empty for a month and he could have rented it to the other people." Benson turned back toward me. "The man, when he get a hand on the money, he don't turn it loose."

"How much," I said.

"A hundred dollars," Benson said.

"I can't," I said. "I don't have a hundred dollars." Truer words were never spoken. I didn't have a hundred dollars. I didn't have fifty dollars. Benson leaned back into the light well, looking up the central shaft.

"Then I don't know what we going to do," he said.

"I know what I'm going to do," I said. "I'm going to talk to Lubin."

"You can talk to him," Benson said. "I don't think he going to change."

Lubin's office was on the fourth floor of another building on Broadway, near the el train tracks. The sign on the door said Marcus and Neumann Realty. The hallway was painted institutional green and there was a mezuzah attached to the door frame of the office. I knocked, and a man cracked the door open and peered out. He had on thick glasses, a yarmulke, and a black coat with white tassels peeping out from under it. His face was pale, milky, and childish.

"Mr. Lubin?" I said.

"Out," said the face behind the crack. The mouth was red and spoke as if it were full of something unpleasant. "Come back two-thirty." The door slammed. I waited in the hallway, smoking cigarettes and stubbing them out, with a degree of malicious pleasure, on the freshly painted walls. I was on the point of grinding the last one into the mezuzah when Lubin finally walked out of the elevator.

He was an older man with a long whitening beard. He wore a wide-brimmed hat down the hallway, and when he took it off there was, of course, a yarmulke underneath it.

I sat down in front of his desk and told him my name and the number of the apartment, and waved my copy of the cashier's check under his nose. Lubin started leafing through some papers and I looked out the window. I could see a train coming down off the bridge and turning onto the el track. Every car was covered with graffiti and the train was as colorful as a king snake.

"Yes," Lubin said, reading from a computer print-out. "You pay your deposit. You pay your one month rent. So what is the problem?"

"The problem is that somebody wants some more money," I said. "According to what I hear, you rented this apartment to two different people."

Lubin looked up at the ceiling, where there were a couple of dead flies hanging in a spider web. The whole office was about half the size of a subway car. Lubin broke abruptly into a long loud tirade about apartments standing empty, people not paying rent, damage to buildings, losses of money.

"Look," I said. "I'm not interested in these things. You got my money anyway. I don't care what your problems are."

"I took the deposit," Lubin said. "But that doesn't mean I have to give you the apartment. I could give back the deposit."

"Sure," I said. "Give it back."

"Wait," Lubin said. "Wait. You want the apartment?"

"Sure I want the apartment," I said. "That's why I paid for it."

"Yes," Lubin said. "Wait and I will talk to Benson. I'm not sure I know what it is you're talking about. Come back again tomorrow."

I went out and walked around the block, thinking it over. It seemed fairly certain that someone was trying to clip me, but I wasn't quite sure who it was. I also couldn't decide whether it was worth fighting it or not. If I could come up with the hundred dollars it would save me trouble and headaches. Evans owed me two hundred, which would be free money if only I could get it. I came back around the corner onto Broadway and went to the wall phone in the dairy restaurant. I slung the receiver over my shoulder and started unloading pieces of paper out of my wallet, looking for Evans's number. A tape came on the line and started telling me, "Please hang up, there appears to be a receiver off the hook, please hang up . . ." etcetera, etcetera, before I found the right scrap. Since it was a call to Jersey it cost me forty cents. But Evans answered on the third ring.

I mentioned my name and Evans burst into a coughing fit, which sounded genuine, and bad. When it was over I said, "Look, Mr. Evans, I've been waiting to get that deposit back, and I was just wondering if it might have been lost in the mail."

"I didn't mail it," Evans said through the phlegm. A train came down on the tracks overhead and I lost the rest of what he was saying.

"What was that?" I said.

"I said what about the piano?" Evans said. "What about the refrigerator, and the broken furniture, and all the stuff on the stairs? The place is a wreck, I can't give you the deposit back. Not until the place is clean."

"Wait a second," I said. "None of that stuff is my stuff. Most of that stuff has been there for years. I never put it there. It was there when I took the place."

"I never put it there either," Evans said. "You're the tenant and you're responsible. Please understand, I can't return the deposit with the place in that condition." Even while ripping me off, Evans still had nice manners.

"I don't understand at all," I said. "I don't see what you're complaining about. Some of those things are worth money. I'm giving it to you all for nothing. You're the first landlord I ever heard complain about an extra refrigerator. That refrigerator *works*, Mr. Evans."

Mr. Evans coughed some more. "Well, the refrigerator," he said. "But what about the piano? I can't turn the place over to my buyer with things like that sitting around."

"Why not?" I said. "It's a nice piano. The guy can have his wife play him music at night." But I knew that was the wrong approach. "You could sell the piano," I said. "Make some extra cash on the whole deal."

"I'm not a junk man," Evans said. "I don't sell pianos. If it's worth anything, then you sell it. And all the rest has got to go too. I'm sorry, but that's my last word. Clean the apartment, you get your deposit. I wrote the check and it's sitting in my desk."

"Wait a second," I said. But the operator came on asking for more change and I didn't have any more change, so the connection was broken.

So I went on the street again and walked up and down, trying to think of a good idea. But as far as I could determine, I was in an airtight box. To make matters worse, it was raining in Brooklyn, right down the back of my neck. And if it was only a tiny bit colder, this rain would be sleet. And if something didn't give, I was going to be sitting out in the weather by the first of the month. I didn't have any illusions that Evans would let me coast into November. If I didn't move to Brooklyn, I would be moving into Grand Central Station. Therefore, I decided, something had to give. Since I didn't know which wall of the box was the weakest, I was going to bang on them all.

That let me in for a busy week. The same afternoon I invested about half of the remains of my petty cash in subway tokens, which I stored in the lining of my coat. When I got back to Hoboken I started calling Evans on the telephone. I was very polite to him, but I called him back every hour, from six until midnight. By the third call Evans was beginning to sound annoyed, which pleased me greatly — I wanted to make a nuisance of myself. At midnight he took his phone off the hook and I went to bed and lay there hoping that he would lose a lot of sleep listening to the telephone company pleading with him to put his receiver back on his phone, and in the morning I got up and rode out to Brooklyn, picking up the latest *Voice* when I changed trains, so that while I was taking a break from trying to drive Benson and Lubin out of their respective minds, which was how I planned to spend the rest of the week, I could keep looking for a job.

I decided to hit Benson first, since I knew Lubin wouldn't be in till two-thirty and I didn't feel like talking to the mush-mouthed mole that shared his office, so I walked down to 185 Broadway and let myself into the building and rang Benson's bell. His wife came to the door, gave me a bright smile full of gold teeth, and said, "Super no here," her only English phrase. She shut the door and I sat down on the stairs across the hall to wait for Benson and mark ads in the newspaper. I was down to the restaurant and security jobs. Freelancing couldn't save me now; I was going to have to do straight time, forty hours a week and the check on Friday. In an hour Benson still hadn't come back and I had circled many ads, so I walked up to the dairy restaurant and got on the telephone, trying to find a place that would hire me immediately or at least before the end of the week. I called the security places first on the theory that that kind of job might be somewhat less dismal than a job in a restaurant. One place, a retail store in Manhattan, said they would take me at once if I fit their bill, so I made an appointment with the manager for the following day. None of the uniformed guard suppliers could promise me anything before the end of November, by which time I would already be dead, but I made appointments with them too, for the next week, and wrote

them all down in my date book so as not to forget. Then I
called Evans once for luck, getting nowhere again, and went
back down Broadway to look for Benson.

I rang his bell and his wife came to the door and turned
around and called into the apartment, "Lo Americano,
Americano." Benson came out in the hall and we had a conversation in which I learned that the hypothetical other
people were named Martinez and they would not take less
than a hundred dollars and they would not take it on the
instalment plan and it would be no use for me to go see them
myself since none of them spoke English. While we were
standing in the hall about a dozen people came up to talk to
Benson about things that weren't working, until Benson
finally turned his palms up in the air at me and ran off to fix
a few things. I went back up to Lubin's office and had a re-
play of my previous day's meeting with him and then I went
back to 185 Broadway and followed Benson around some
more and then I went back to Hoboken and called Evans
every hour and listened to him cough and choke over the
phone until it was bedtime.

The next day I got up and put on my clean shirt and my
tie and my jacket with the barely noticeable hole in the left
elbow and went to keep my appointment at the store, which
turned out to be a sort of budget boutique in the East Village.
I went in a donut shop across the street and sat in front of
one cup of coffee for around forty minutes, to be sure I
arrived at exactly the right time, and then I went over and
talked to the floor manager. I filled out the standard applica-
tion and discussed the duties of the job with the manager and
told him all about how I loved the store and the job and the
manager himself and how eager I was to get the job and
start working right away, with overtime if possible. I must
have made the right impression, because the manager, who
was actually a little twit, said that he wanted to take me,
only first I had to take a polygraph test, because that was

routine for all employees. So he called up a snoop shop in midtown and made an appointment between me and the machine for Friday; he couldn't get it any sooner.

So I wrote the appointment in my date book like a good little businessman, and I got out of there. I went around the corner and stepped into a doorway and changed my clothes out of the shoulder bag I was carrying, so I wouldn't look like I was worth mugging when I went out to Brooklyn, which was what I planned to do next. Then I went to Brooklyn and rang Benson's bell and his wife came and said, "Super no here," and I hung around in the hallways till I caught him, and we talked more about the Martinez family, and I visited Lubin again and I went home and called Evans all night, and this went on for the rest of the week, and nothing gave an inch.

During this time I formed the idea that if I could somehow catch Benson and Lubin together I might be able to break them down. Or at least I could find out which one of them was trying to con me, which was something I wanted to know more and more, if only for the satisfaction of knowing. But of course Lubin wouldn't come down to the building, and Benson wouldn't go up to the office. Patience was the obvious answer, but I had too little time to waste it on patience. But I still hadn't got them together when Friday came and I had to go keep my appointment at O.Q.R. Security Systems.

O.Q.R. was a typical operation of its kind. They ran uniformed guards out the front door and private eyes out the back and somewhere in the middle they had a polygraph machine to keep tabs on both ends of the business. I walked into their waiting room and talked to the receptionist through a hole in the wall the size of a matchbox. She pushed a twenty-page questionnaire through the hole at me and told me to sit down and fill it out and wait. I took the form to a chair and looked it over, and it was asking a lot of questions I really couldn't afford to answer. I hadn't expected anything like it. I had expected to be asked about drug addiction and felony convictions, two problems I happened not to have, and here were all these questions about problems that I did have. But I was up there already so I decided to try it. I filled out the form with what I wished was the truth and waited for them to call me. I sat there hoping that polygraph tests really are as unreliable as statistics say they are.

Then the examiner came for me. He was a young man on the make and he was wearing a Qiana shirt, open wide enough to show his gold chains, and he had a cute little pistol clipped to the back of his belt, right under the small of his back. We went in the examination room and we shook hands and he showed me the machine and asked me a lot of irrelevant questions that were supposed to help me relax, and then he had to go take a phone call, so I got a chance to look around the room. It looked like the inside of a refrigerator. There weren't any windows, but there was a big mirror. I went to the mirror and cupped my hands around my eyes so I could see into the little closet behind it, but no one was there. I sat back down.

The examiner came back and started plugging me into the apparatus. He put an air-pressure sleeve on my arm to read my heart rate, and clips on my fingers for my galvanic skin response, and two tubes around my chest for my breathing. Then he warned me not to move. If I moved the machine would get upset, he told me. He went back to the control panel and flipped some switches and four needles began to trace all my thoughts and feelings onto a large rotating spool of paper. I was then asked a lot of questions. I answered some of them truthfully and lied my face off on others. It all took about twenty minutes. When it was over the examiner got me untangled from the equipment and I stood up and asked him how I did. He apologized and said that professional ethics forbade him to tell me that, but he wished me the best. So I wished him the best, and we smiled and shook hands some more, and I went out of the office and got into the elevator.

Back in the street it was beginning to get dark. Everyone was getting off work, and I walked into a crowd and let it carry me all around the midtown area. Eventually the crowd spat me out in Herald Square, which is a concrete triangle where Broadway meets Sixth Avenue. There are benches there and winos and drug dealers and a big subway nexus and Macy's is right across the street. I sat down on a bench next to a guy who was passed out. His coat had fallen open and he didn't have anything on underneath it. I decided he was dead and moved to another bench. It should have been dusk, but twilight doesn't happen in midtown Manhattan; all the city lights go on and push the lingering daylight up into the stratosphere or down below 14th Street. At one end of the square there was a statue of Horace Greeley. At the other end there was a clock. It was twenty to six. They had told me at the store that I could call after six and find out if I got the job or not, but I was already sure I had flunked the polygraph test. I decided I was dead. But even a snake will keep on squirming after it's been cut in half. I picked up a scrap of newspaper to read while I waited for after six to come. It was a Spanish paper and after I had looked at it for a few minutes I realized it was some sort of Dear Abby column. I could make out verbs and prepositions but not the nouns, so I wasn't quite sure what the Spanish people's problems were, or how they were going to get solved. But because the column was impossible to understand it kept me amused for a nice long time.

Then it was after six and I got up and started looking for a good pay phone. Herald Square was littered with them, but I didn't want to call the store from the street, because then they would know I was on the street. I walked down Sixth Avenue, looking into coffee shops, but none of them had phones for some reason, so I went into a bar. It was quiet enough and I made the call and the girl who answered the phone told me that I had the job. Nothing about the polygraph test, just that I had the job and I should show up on Monday. I hung up the phone. There were only a couple of people in the bar, watching television. My heart was breaking for a drink, but luckily I had nothing in my pockets but tokens and a few dimes. I went to Brooklyn.

This time I didn't even ring Benson's bell. I just sat down on the steps opposite his door, with my chin in my hands and my elbows on my knees. I wasn't sure if I wanted to see Benson or not and I thought I would let luck decide. Some time went by and luck sent Benson in through the double front doors.

"How you doing good?" Benson said. He was an optimist, in his own way.

"Got a job," I said. Benson gave me congratulations. I asked him why he had a suit on, and he said he was coming from church.

"I got a job," I said, after we had had some conversation. "I start it Monday. I'm not sure I'm going to have time to be a Ping-Pong ball for you and Lubin anymore."

"Well," said Benson. "You going to kick it out?"

"Maybe," I said. "Who do I give it to? Lubin?"

"Don't give it to Lubin," Benson said. "Lubin keep it if you do. It got to go to the people."

"The people," I said.

"Martinez," Benson said.

"How do I give money to these people," I said. "I never even saw them."

"Bring it to me," Benson said. "I get it to them."

I looked at Benson. I was sitting on the first landing and

Benson was standing on the hall floor and he looked very small down there. He stared back at me for something like a minute. Then he turned aside and looked out through the double glass doors. Benson smiled as though he had recognized someone, and I craned my head to see who it was, but the street was empty.

"One time," Benson said to the glass doors, "I lie to someone. To a man. A long time ago." Then he was silent for another minute. I looked at the street and noticed that it was raining again. The pavement was black and glossy with the rain.

"I never told him," I heard Benson say. "Not for a long time. And the lie came back at me. All the time, it coming back at me. Because if you lie, you have to live with it all by yourself, with your lie. And I don't like to live all by myself."

The pavement was so wet that I could see a traffic light reflecting in it. First it was red and then it was green. The colors swirled in the water.

"So then I went to the man," Benson said. "To tell him. And he laughed at me, because by then it was years, and he said, 'All this time passing, and you coming here now to tell me this?' He don't know why, but I had to tell him. So I don't have it with me no more."

A car came down the street and broke up the reflected light and water splashed on the outer door.

"I had to tell him," Benson said. I had the feeling he didn't know I was there anymore, so I lit a cigarette and kept quiet until I finished it.

"I'll bring the money," I said. "By Sunday, if I can."

"Good," Benson said. "You find me here on Sunday." I went out through the doors and walked up to the train, hugging the buildings so I wouldn't get too wet. I had decided, now. I didn't really believe in the Martinez family but now I thought that maybe I could believe in Benson. That would make it Lubin's play somehow, but I didn't even want to think about it; I was tired of thinking about it and of not trusting anyone. I went home and by Sunday there I was with my hundred bucks and a rented van containing my mattress and etceteras. I bought the key from Benson and moved my stuff into my apartment. Benson had patched the walls and painted and the place was clean and white. I pushed my mattress up against the radiator and lay down on it and let the steam heat sing me to sleep.

Then on Monday I started the job, and I couldn't get off on a weekday till the following week, so I couldn't get up to Lubin's office to sign my lease. The delay didn't bother me much. Now that I was in the place no piece of paper was going to get me out. But I did want to see Lubin again to nag him about the hundred dollars, so I went up there the first chance I got. From my new position of security, I was considering holding back a piece of the next month's rent.

So I went up to the office and there was no new trouble. Lubin and I each signed a few copies of the lease and I folded one up and put it in my coat pocket.

"So," Lubin said. "You like the apartment?" His English was thick and heavily accented. It was probably his third language, after Hebrew and Yiddish, and doubtless the least important to him. The Hasidim just don't believe that anybody else is really there.

"Too expensive," I said.

"So?" Lubin said. "You take it, you leave it." He smiled in his beard. "You took it."

"Not the rent," I said. "The kickback. A hundred dollars, that's expensive."

"What?" Lubin said. He sat up and looked very surprised. "Benson took a hundred dollars?" I looked at him. There was no doubting it. I had never seen Lubin look so sincere. Probably it was because he hadn't got a cut.

"It's too much," Lubin said. "Twenty dollars, thirty dollars, yes, but this is too much. I will speak with Benson."

I looked out the window. For just a minute I felt very upset. It was so simple to give the lie to Lubin, and now I couldn't do that. I had lost track of the lie now, and I might never find it again. Out beyond the window I could see the bright ribbon of train tracks curling away over the bridge, gleaming in the afternoon sun. So maybe the lie was out there too, I thought, even if I couldn't see it. It was just there, floating around with the other particles of the atmosphere, and everybody got a little piece of it, and it didn't belong to anyone. And that was fair for everybody, even for me. Because after all the hundred dollars didn't come from nowhere.

"Don't say anything to Benson," I told Lubin. "It's over now anyway. And I have to live with him."

I left Lubin's office and walked around my new neighborhood, looking into groceries and liquor stores and views and other matters of interest. And I thought a little bit about the hundred dollars, which, finally, I had squeezed out of Evans. I spent the whole Saturday before I started the job cleaning out the old apartment. I got rid of almost a truckload of junk and got a ticket for littering the street, which was a very funny thing to get a ticket for in Hoboken. Then in the evening I lured Evans out to the place to look at everything I had done. He was gratified, but he was still complaining about the piano and the refrigerator and all the broken furniture I hadn't been able to move.

So then I went into high gear. I gave Evans a recital of my sad situation, and I made a real tear-jerker out of it. It was very poetic and would have brought blood from a stone. It began with when I last ate and ended with when I expected to eat again, and there was a great deal of material in the middle. When it was over, Evans removed his glasses and wiped them and told me that he too knew what suffering was, because he had just found out he had cancer, and he was going into the hospital the following week and he didn't know if he would ever come back out. So then we commiserated with each other and Evans wrote me a new check, for the whole two hundred dollars. He gave it to me in exchange for my faithful promise that I would find some salvage company to remove all the stuff, but of course I never did anything of the kind.

I deposited Evans's check and held my breath till it cleared the bank. By that time it was no longer safe for me to go to Hoboken. I had been defaulting on my utility bills for quite some time, and I was afraid they were going to get me. The electric bill hadn't been paid for about a year before I even moved into the place, and I knew Evans would weep for real when he found out about that, as he was sure to eventually, when the building finally changed hands. But the most immediate problem was that I owed a big fine for littering. It was time to disappear, obviously, and that is just what I did.

I never went back to Hoboken, not even to drop off my key, and so I never knew if Evans lived or died. I still have the key, as a matter of fact, and sometimes I think about Evans, with his wet glasses and his nice professorial manners and his ruined buildings and his incurable cough. He wasn't a bad person, in his own way, and at least he didn't stop the check. Or maybe he died and didn't have a chance to stop it. I don't know, but sometimes I do wonder if he lived long enough to go back to the apartment and find out that I conned him. I'm sure he's dead by now either way, since you don't live too long without your lungs, so it really doesn't matter at all. But sometimes I still catch myself wondering.

I ♥ NY

❖

ALL OVER the *New York Post*, people are starting to get involved. I'm always seeing the headlines —

IRT RIDERS CAPTURE TRAIN BANDIT, HOLD TIL COPS ARRIVE
&
WOMAN KO'S ATTACKER WITH BRICK
or
CITIZEN CROWD NABS TIMES SQUARE MUGGER

"I really can't believe it," Patrolman Krepacki, a native of Greenpoint, was quoted as saying. "Twenty years on the force, I didn't see anything like this." Things are looking up in the city. The *Post* proudly reports the passage of a tough new gun law in Albany. Death by violence will now decline. The millennium will continue on page 6. Also, I personally expect, peonies are going to start sprouting up in the cracks in the sidewalk on Delancey Street, and everything is going to get real nice, real soon. The other day I went to Kodak in Cooper Square to pick up some film stock for a friend. I put the film in my shoulder bag and went to see a double feature on Second Avenue. When the movies were over I was hungry and went over to Ray's on Prince

Street. I ate an Italian sausage with green peppers and grease baked in pizza dough. They call this a SoHo Roll, for some reason I don't know, and it cost $1.65. Anyway I didn't feel hungry anymore after I had eaten it all. I went outside and began walking across Prince Street through the garbage and broken glass. It was late and everything was quiet except for the bass line shaking the steel door of the after-hours club by the corner of Elizabeth. Across the street the beggars were sleeping sweetly in the mouth of a burned-out building that the city was going to seal five years ago. Everything was as it should be or usually is. I came to the Bowery and stopped for a traffic light. Across the Bowery two bums were fighting in a doorway. Two bums are always fighting in a doorway at the corner of Prince and the Bowery at half-past midnight on Tuesdays and no one ever takes any interest because it doesn't mean anything at all. But as I watched from my corner I thought I detected signs of malicious intent, and I decided to cross over and poke my nose in. This I began to do. But the light was still red and when I got to the median there was a line of cars coming uptown and I had to wait for the line to go by. Meanwhile the action in the doorway seemed to be taking on the shape of a mugging. A big man and a little man were wrestling. The little man appeared to be wearing a tan suit coat. While I stood on the median looking over the stream of cars the big man forced this coat down over the little man's elbows and finally took it away from him altogether. Then he began to walk up the street, holding the coat by the collar, shaking it, dipping his hands into the pockets. Meanwhile the last car in the line stopped at my feet. I looked and saw that it was a police car. There were two cute young cops inside, just like the ones on *Adam 12*. The one on the passenger side had a black mustache and the one driving had a blond mustache and was looking at me inquiringly. Hey, I said, there's a mugging taking place right across the street. The police car went in gear and shot off uptown at sixty miles an hour. This was demoralizing. I could now get across the street, but the magic moment in which I might have done something had receded into the past while I was stuck on the median. The mugger and the muggee were separated, both walking up toward Houston Street with a little distance between them. I watched the mugger. It was offensive to me how slow he was walking. If you are going to rob someone you might have the politeness to run away afterward. I walked along behind the two people, thinking about this last proposition. Opposite Stanton Street there is a parking lot enclosed in a storm fence. Guard dogs run behind the fence at night. They maul you first and ask questions later. By the time the mugger got to this parking lot he was through with the coat, and he threw it over the fence and kept on walking at the same pace, whistling a little now, and swinging his arms. The muggee stopped by the parking lot and stood watching the dogs eat his coat. He looked very unhappy. I passed him without saying hello. There were several other people walking around on the street, but they did not seem to have seen anything. I kept following the mugger, who I had decided was someone to dislike. He went into a bar at the corner of Houston Street. I have been in the bar many times. There is a small pool table and sometimes I go and play for dollar bills with the bums and small-time criminals that hang around in there. It is a good place to hustle dollar bets but not a good place to initiate vigilante action, I don't think. I took a good look at the mugger through the grimy plate glass as I walked past the bar to the corner. I didn't picture myself going home just then, though I had no particular plans. I thought I might make a telephone call, but there was a dearth of pay phones in the area. The nearest one was inside the bar but that one didn't tempt me. I looked east on Houston Street and saw an inviting little blue and white light down by the F train stop on Second

Avenue. I went over there and punched 911 on the keyboard.
The telephone was ringing. A woman's voice answered.
Hello, I said, I just saw a mugging on the Bowery and the
guy who did it went into a bar here and I think he might be
there for a while. How long ago, the woman said. Five
minutes maybe, I said. Can you describe the perpetrator, she
said. No, I said, I'll describe me. I am a white male with
short brown hair and a black jacket with a hole in the back
and blue pants and a brown shoulder bag with seven hundred
dollars' worth of film in it that I don't want to lose, and I'll
be waiting for the car on the southwest corner of Bowery
and Houston. I hung up. During the two and a half minutes
I was on the telephone a fight had broken out in the bar and
when I came back to the Bowery the fight was all over the
street. It was a bum's fight, a lot of shouting and not much
real contact, but still confusing, and there were a lot of
people in it. I didn't see the perpetrator and I wasn't sure if
he was still inside or not. I crossed to the west side of the
street and looked around from there. The perpetrated-upon
had given up on his coat and gone away, apparently, or anyway I couldn't see him anymore. I stood on the corner for
seven minutes. The car with the two mustaches in it came
back and pulled over. Fella, we didn't see any mugging,
the two mustaches said, all we saw was two guys walking
on the street. So why didn't you talk to me? I said. Anyway,
the mustaches said, can you describe the guy you say did
something. Yes, I said, he's Latin, late twenties it looks like,
curly hair and a black mustache, got on a denim jacket and
denim pants and I think he's in that bar across the street.
You saw him go in there? the mustaches said. Yes, I said, but
he could have come out while I was making the call. The
mustaches looked at the bar. The fight was over and everybody was going back inside. What about the other guy? the
mustaches said. Oh yeah, I said, he's older, middle-aged guy,
Latin too, I think. Has on dark polyester pants and a white

shirt, straight hair with a bald spot in the back. He must have gone south or I would have seen him pass. The two mustaches buzzed at each other for a minute. I think I know that guy, the blond mustache said. We're gonna ride downtown and see if we see him. You want me to wait here for you to come back? I said. I wouldn't do that if I were you, they said. The car pulled out and drove downtown. I walked down to the corner of Prince and sat in a doorway. In the next door over a wino was sitting with his head between his legs, talking to his left shoe, which didn't have any laces. I looked up at the sky between the buildings but there was nothing to see up there. I watched the bar. No one came out that I had ever seen before. I was sleepy. After a short time the police car came back. It stopped outside the bar for a minute and then drove on past. I understood that it had only stopped for the traffic light. I got up and switched the bag with the film in it to my left shoulder and walked down to Delancey. In the door of Bob's Smoke Shop there was a tall black hooker with white spandex pants on. She started for me, but I went down the stairs to the station. There is always water dripping somewhere in the J stop on the Bowery. I looked in the trash and found some scraps of the *Post* to read. John Travolta had gone to Magique with an unidentified mystery date. Ramsey Clark was perhaps going to be prosecuted for going to Iran. Subway tokens were going to cost more on the first of July. When the train came I threw down the paper and got in the front car. I stood in the door so I could look down the tunnel. It gives me the vertigo and helps me forget things. The train picks up speed after Essex Street, racing out of the tunnel and up the grade of the bridge. I see the lights of the project towers blurring by on both sides. In the middle of the bridge the train slows down. Sometimes there are barges and tugs on the river. I can also see the building I live in when the train gets near the Brooklyn side. Sometimes there are fires in the area, and I can see these very well from the train. The train goes five blocks past my building, and I get off at the first stop and walk back, into the stiff breeze that is usually blowing back off the river.

Not much was going on in the neighborhood. The kids came every morning and played disco under my windows. Someone tried to break into my apartment but I came home in time and he had to run away. I spend most of my time sleeping or reading tabloids. I read the *Post* and the *News* and sometimes the *Enquirer* or one of the other big national trash papers. The *Post* has always been my favorite, though. I told everybody about what happened on the Bowery. Soon they got bored with it. After all, this is the city, I was told. Things happen. You should get a regular job and stop sitting around being morbid. Your problem is that you don't do anything, my girlfriend told me. You're right, I said. I think I'll start growing a beard. I don't think you're funny, she said. I think you're becoming a bore. Also you never have any money. True enough, I reflected. I decided to go to Career Blazers. I was in the front car of the F train. There were no pretty girls in the car. There was a young woman sitting across from me but she was too tall and too thin and the tendons on her neck were overdeveloped. Even her hair looked brittle and nervous. I began reading the *Post*. A woman had managed to fend off a gang of muggers on a subway in Queens. She was an immigrant from Poland. In the picture she looked stolid and able to withstand everything. There were bandages around her head because she had been hurt in the fighting. Elsewhere in the paper, Koch and Carey were mad at each other again. Someone threw a banana peel at Koch while he was marching in a Puerto Rican parade. A Puerto Rican politician caught the banana peel before it hit Koch. A rare photo had been taken of Woody Allen. According to the caption, Allen attacked the photographer after the picture was taken. There was also a picture of several Harlem teenagers being arrested on suspicion of robbing subway passengers. Suspect Mugs For Camera, the caption said. The suspect was indeed mugging for the camera, in a model's pose, with one hand on her hip and the other handcuffed to a transit officer. She was black and her features were obscured by the grain of the photograph, except for her teeth, which seemed very white. She had on a T-shirt which also looked white in the photograph. SASSON! the T-shirt said. Across the car from me a man rolled out of his seat and hit the floor. The woman who wasn't quite pretty bent over him. Her neck was tense with nervous concern. The two of them didn't seem to be personally acquainted. I folded the paper and got up and snatched the man by the shoulders and put him back on his seat. He was much heavier than I had expected. The seat next to him was vacant and I sat down on it. The heavy man tipped into me like a barrel falling over. I pushed him upright and looked in his face. What's wrong, I said, are you sick, do you want to go to a doctor, did you take something, what are you taking? Talk to me. I tried to shake him but he was too solid to shake. I took a look at his eyes. They didn't look like the eyes of a drugged person. As I watched them, the eyes came into focus. They killed my wife, the man said with emphasis. The woman who wasn't quite pretty took a deep breath. The train was pulling into the 14th Street station. Let's get off the train, I said, and go to Saint Vincent's Hospital. You want to do that? He seemed to want to do that a lot. He got up and pitched onto the floor again. The doors opened and he began to crawl toward the doors on his hands and knees. I tried to lift him up, but he was really very heavy. I could see the feet of people entering and leaving the train. The heavy man stood halfway up when he got to the doors. He made it just in time to get his arms caught in them as they closed. *Please clear the doors in the front car,* the public address system said. *This train cannot proceed until the doors are closed*. Other people began to come forward to render assistance. The doors were pried open and I danced off the train, holding the heavy man around the waist. So far we were still on our feet. When we got out he began to slump forward again and I raised my arms and put him in a full nelson, that being the easiest way to hold him up. Helpful hands threw my *Post* and a paper bag full of something onto the platform. The doors closed and the train began to pull out. There was a lot of metal and glass going by very rapidly under my nose. The heavy man was so short that his head fit very neatly under my chin. The train stopped being there and I saw the wall on the opposite side of the track. In a moment my eyes adjusted to the fact that the wall was not moving. Now the heavy man seemed to be holding his own weight up, so I bent over and re-trieved the *Post* and the paper bag. He took the paper bag from me and stuck it in his right armpit. Why did they have to take her? he said. I didn't say anything. Why are you doing this? he said. I didn't try to answer that one either. He began to cry a little and his legs started to spin out. I got an arm under his shoulders and began to walk him up the first stairway. But he was really shockingly heavy, con-sidering that he wasn't really fat. I was afraid I might lose him and he would hurt himself falling. I began trying to persuade him to sit down so I could go make a phone call. He didn't want to sit down, though. He leaned into the stair rail and began to unload pieces of paper out of his pockets. He picked out a yellow piece and shoved it at me. The slip had been folded ten times over and it was torn along every fold. It took me some time to get it open. When I did I saw that it was the death certificate of a woman named Sandra Lorenzo. The place of death was listed as some subway station in Brooklyn I never heard of. The cause of death was listed as acute trauma of the clavicle complicated by contusions of the scapula, or something like that, death from being beaten to death, in layman's terms. The date of the death certificate was November 19. It was now May. This was November, I said to Lorenzo, what's wrong with you lately? I can't get over it, he said. I guess you can't get over it, I said. I wish I had something to say to you. Where are you going? Beth Israel, he said. You know how to get there? I said. I know, Lorenzo said, and he went up a step under his own power. He turned around and put his hands on my shoulders. Our eyes were level now. His hands felt strong. Thank you, thank you, he said. Don't follow me. Get back on the train. I watched him go up the stairs and through the gate. He didn't look so bad, only a little unsteady. I went down the stairs to wait for the next F train. It was very bright there at the north end of the platform. No one else was waiting and for some reason the platform reminded me of a hospital corridor at four in the morning. Even the tiles on the wall looked clean. And Beth Israel wasn't within a mile of that end of 14th Street. I ran out of the station. On the street corner there was a man standing. He looked like a European model, a Louis Jourdan type but blond. Have you been here long? I said to him. Did you happen to notice — But he was already denying everything and running away. I found Lorenzo on 16th Street. He was headed east and weaving badly, also he had a handful of dollar bills which he was waving around in the open. This in particular looked bad to me. I caught up with him. Please, I said, let's go to Saint Vincent's. Beth Israel, he said. That's nowhere near here, I said, let me go with you. I'm meeting people taking me there, he said. So let me go with you to meet them, I said. Look at you, you're all over the street. Something bad is going to happen to you. I love you and I respect you, Lorenzo said, please go get back on the train. All right then, I said, but at least put your money in your pocket before somebody comes along and takes it away from you. I began to back away. When I was clear I turned around and went back down into the station. There was a transit cop on the mezzanine and I went up to him. Are you only a transit cop, I said, or do you also go in the street? What you got going? he said. There's a guy who's crazy, I said. In November someone killed his wife. He says he can't get over it. He's all over 16th Street waving money around in the air. He thinks he's going to Beth Israel. What's he look like? the cop said. Short and stocky, real heavyset, I said. Black hair, short and straight. Brown eyes, and he's got on a striped shirt with a button-down collar and a paper sack he's carrying under his arm. Looks like he might be Italian. I think his name's Lorenzo, I called after the cop, who was headed up to the street. He showed me his wife's death certificate, I said to the air. Down below I could hear a train coming. I went down and got on the train and rode all the way to Queens Plaza without being able to think of what I had been planning to do that day. So I caught another train and went home. I thought it might be fun to look in old newspapers and see if there was anything about the brutal murder of Sandra Lorenzo, survived and mourned by devoted and broken-hearted Victor or Francesco or whatever. But however lackluster my housekeeping was, I didn't still have *Post*s from November in May.

I had cockroaches in my telephone. Whenever I made a call some roaches would roll out from under the dial, like tiny paratroopers bailing out of an aircraft hatch. I had some mice too, in the kitchen. One day I saw this mouse that was so big it was almost a rat. When I shooed at it it just sat there giving me this what-are-*you*-doing-here look. Then it slouched off under the sink. I went in to Canal Street to get some poison but when I got there it was raining and I didn't feel like looking for it anymore. I didn't want to go home again either so I was just wandering around in the drizzle.

I drifted up to Delancey Street and finally walked past both subway stops till I was near the foot of the bridge. I had on cloth shoes and my feet were wet and I thought I would probably catch cold. There is a newsstand there on the corner of Clinton and I thought I would just buy the papers and go home and get in bed and read them. There were a lot of people crowded under the awning of the newsstand to get out of the rain and all of them were pushing me. There was a cop leaning over the counter asking for a copy of *Consumer Reports*. A Latin woman was trying to get his attention. Someone is just now taking my purse, she was saying, with my cards and my money. She was about four feet tall and dumpy and dressed in a damp cotton sack dress and she had a big mole on the corner of her mouth. The cop dodged away from her and went to the other end of the counter. The woman followed him. My cards and all my money, she said. Also my umbrella which I am buying only today. Go to the precinct and report it, the cop said. Gimme a copy of *Consumer Reports*, the one with the 1980 cars in it. The woman went out and stood on the northwest corner of Clinton Street. Raindrops accumulated in her hair. I went up to her. Do you still see him? I said. Yes, yes, she said. He is over there. She pointed. With my cards, my money, and my umbrella which is new. I do not know where is the precinct, she said. On the other side of Delancey there was a young Latin guy hurrying down Clinton. You're sure about this, I said. It is my new umbrella which he is holding now in his hand. My purse he has thrown already away. But my cards and my money, those he still must have. The light changed and I trotted across the street. I took no time to consider. If I considered I knew I would do nothing. I caught up with the guy by the vacant lot on the next corner. He had a short Afro and a dirty blue Windbreaker, and in his right hand he was holding a folding umbrella of the kind that you buy for two dollars on any street corner ten minutes before it rains. The umbrella was shut. I once studied karate for several years, though I have never done any street fighting. To be a good fighter one must have a mind empty of conscious thought and I am ordinarily inhibited by an excess of imagination. But today my mind seemed to be as empty as a crater on the moon. It must be the rain, I thought, and I hit the guy on the left shoulder. I hit him with the heel of my hand, hard enough to spin him. He came around very quickly, swiping with the umbrella, which was a logical thing to expect. I stepped outside and hit his wrist with a single-arm block and the umbrella flew away somewhere. Now his left hand was coming toward my face, but slowly enough that I could catch it. I held his hand, turned it up and inward in a loop which puts pressure on the wrist, the elbow, and the shoulder. This is a technique from aikido. I don't really know any aikido, but a guy I met in the park once showed me this trick. He also talked to me about the philosophy of aikido, which is quite complicated, having to do with circles and so on. This particular trick is supposed to be unbearably painful. The alleged purse snatcher went to his knees on the wet sidewalk. Aaah, he said. You must be crazy, bro. I didn't stop. I had forgotten why I was doing this but I didn't seem to be able to stop. Rain water was running out of my hair into my eyes and mouth. I remembered about the umbrella and turned my head to look for it. The Latin woman was stumping along toward us on her swollen wet feet. I watched her pick up the umbrella. Is not my umbrella, she said. My umbrella was with flowers. She came closer, bent over and peered at the stranger I was torturing on the sidewalk. Is not the same one, she said, is not the same. I didn't feel up to apologizing. I let go of the guy's hand and stepped back out of range. He stood up, thought it over, and ran away down Clinton Street. I pulled my hair as hard as I could and started back to Delancey. The woman was waddling behind me. She was talking, but to herself, I think, and not to me. Is not the same one, she said regretfully, not the same. They are all looking the same now, the young people. I heard the umbrella pop open. Is not so bad this umbrella, she said, though it is not so beautiful as the other. But it is keeping off the rain. I go now to the precinct to tell of my cards and my money. Probably she was talking to me after all. If she had been talking to herself I suppose it would have been in Spanish. Still I didn't stop or look back. I decided to walk across the bridge so I wouldn't have to think about what had happened. I climbed the stairs to the promenade and began to walk. When I came to the first tower the rain stopped and the sky began to clear. I looked down at the street below the bridge. All the people were coming out onto the street now that the rain had stopped. The people were no bigger than cockroaches and it was true that they did all look the same. Also when I put my hand out over the railing my hand covered all the people up and I couldn't see any of them anymore.

The Forgotten Bridge

◆

I FIRST SAW Angel the first time I went to my new neighborhood at night. I hadn't moved in yet but I had the key in my pocket and I got a sudden impulse to go stand in the place. I took the eastbound J train one stop into Brooklyn and got off. This happened at the end of October and it was already quite cold and windy, as it always is near the river.

I met Angel near the triangle where South 8th Street runs into Broadway. He was just standing there on the sidewalk and when I came up to him he hit me for a cigarette. I was glad to give it to him. Giving out cigarettes makes good neighbors, up to a point. But it took me a while to fish one out, and Angel detected my nervousness, the way they say dogs can smell fear. He tried to get unpleasant, but he was very drunk and I had no trouble shaking him off. The episode left me a touch of bad feeling about the neighborhood but there was already nothing I could do about it. It happened three blocks away from my building and I thought that with luck I would never see Angel again. I didn't know his name yet either, of course.

I was broke when I moved into the apartment. It often happens when you move. I had a slightly negative bank account, so I took a job as a store cop in lower Manhattan.

It was a stupid job but I managed to hold it down for about six weeks.

I went on at ten A.M. and got off usually at seven or eight at night. When I got off I would walk around in the streets for a while and then go home. If I wanted hot food I ate out, because I couldn't afford to put the gas on in the apartment yet. We got two days off a week, but never in a row, and most of the time I was at home I was asleep. I wasn't spending much time in the neighborhood. The only person I knew in the building was the super. Everybody was Spanish but me.

Toward the end of November it began to get very cold in the apartment. There was steam heat but it was all blown out by the wind. I had several windows facing the river and they all leaked so badly that sometimes the breeze inside the apartment would blow my newspapers around. The one broken window I patched with linoleum tiles from the kitchen floor, but I knew I would have to do better than that sometime. It was a long way to summer.

I knew someone in Manhattan who was a painter. One day he found a big roll of canvas on the street. When he got it home he realized that it had been painted with spray paint and so could not be reprimed or repainted. The canvas was a relic of some kind of social worker art project in which they make the street kids paint on canvas instead of on the trains. What they paint looks great on the trains, lousy on canvas. I took the roll of canvas home to Brooklyn.

One night I rolled the canvas out on the floor and began ripping it up into big squares. I took the squares and tacked them over my windows with pushpins and sealed the edges with gaffer's tape. When I had done three windows it was already warmer in the apartment. There were eight windows. When I had done four the doorbell rang for the first time since I had been living there.

Ordinarily I would have sat quietly for half an hour or so

and ignored it. But ripping the canvas made a lot of noise, and I knew that whoever was out there knew I was home. I opened the door. It was two Spanish kids from the neighborhood. They told me their names were Angel and Pollo. They came in and started looking around the room.

There was not a lot to look at. I had no furniture other than a table with a few things on it. I had two big pieces of broken mirror I had found on the street and put up on the wall for company. Also I had put up head shots in a continuous band at eye level all around the apartment.

Head shot is the trade term for an 8-by-10 glossy close-up of an actress. Her résumé is taped to the back. Directors collect notebooks full of these things. Every so often they throw them all away. I found a batch of them on the street and lined them along my walls with black masking tape. I had hoped it would look interesting, a black-and-white continuum of *Glamour* eyes, Miss America smiles. But I didn't like looking at them up on my wall. Their careers were finished anyway. They were garbage. I left them up there because it would have peeled the paint to take them down.

Angel and Pollo liked the head shots. They wanted to know if I had taken the pictures. I told them I didn't have a camera. They were curious about the canvas too, and I told them where it had come from. We went in the kitchen where it was warmer and drank some quarts of beer they had with them. I brought out the last of a bag of dope I had owned for two years or so. I had quit smoking it a long time before and had been carrying the bag around from here to there along with the rest of my household goods — a skillet, a winter coat, some boxes of paper, and the world's first electric typewriter, which weighed a hundred pounds.

Pollo did most of the talking, because his English was better. Sometimes he would translate for Angel. Sometimes Angel would talk for himself. They started looking at the paint, trying to find traces of a fire that had happened in the apartment some time before. It was white latex paint that the super had slapped on so quickly that now if you began peeling it at any one point it would come off the whole wall. We began talking about the super, whose name was Eugenio Benson.

"Bensone," Angel said. "Where he get a name like that? He a nigger from Santo Domingo." Angel was drunk now and I realized for the first time that we had met before. This was also my first encounter with the inverse square law of sectarianism and racial animosity. I liked Benson, even though he had shaken me down for a hundred dollars when I moved in. He had a baby and his wife was pregnant and he got paid two hundred dollars a month. What could he do? He was only five feet tall and it was a big building. I gave him the money. I didn't have any choice either. When the baby came I took his wife a pound of espresso.

I gave Angel and Pollo some leftover head shots when they left. I sealed up the rest of the windows and decided it was good that they came. They had seen that I had nothing, and the word would go out that I wasn't worth breaking into even though I was white. I never told Angel that we had met before and it was plain that he didn't remember. Everything was fine.

On the first of December I got the gas turned on and quit my job. It was getting too crazy to stay there, with the Christmas rush beginning. I still didn't have any money and I spent hours in the public library phone booths, trying to hustle some free-lance work. I went up to Columbia and did psychology experiments for three dollars and carfare. I did many ridiculous things. Finally I managed to collect an old debt and that left me enough to coast into the new year.

When the cold weather really set in the kids began to hang out in the entryway by the mailboxes. At other times they would hang out at a housing project for the elderly that was a few blocks away. When they were there they robbed people, I knew. My peripheral vision improved a great deal that winter, but I didn't have any trouble. It might have been because the news was out that I wasn't worth it. It might have been that Angel and Pollo were graduates of the gang and had people's respect. It might have been for some other reason.

If I ran into Angel and Pollo they would usually hold me talking and give me a little beer. I found out more about them this way. They were cousins. Pollo lived with his mother in the building. His father was dead. Angel lived down the street. He was older and had been in the Marines, stationed in Germany. He could speak German almost as well as English, not very well.

One night we were down in the entryway and a lot of noise was being made. Someone opened a door upstairs and called. Angel and Pollo shut up and ran into a short blind corridor beside the broken elevator. They made me hide there with them. We were very quiet and we could hear heavy feet in slippers coming down the stairs. When the feet reached the first landing I heard asthmatic breathing too. It was Pollo's mother. She cursed us a long time in Spanish, but she didn't want to come down the last flight, and after a while we heard her climbing painfully back up.

Because I was trying hard not to drink during these months, I spent as little time as possible with Angel and Pollo. Even just drinking beer I was afraid I might hit the horror line and if that happened I could easily swallow my entire net worth in two or three days. Once I was visited by a friend from the past and when he left there was most of a quart of Scotch in my house. I spent a week looking at it. I was protected by the fact that I don't like the taste of Scotch, but that wasn't going to last forever. The next time I ran into Angel and Pollo I brought the bottle down to them.

There were some other people there too, and the bottle began to go around. I think Angel and I got most of it in the end. People had beer, which we drank for chasers. Several separate conversations got started. Mine was with Pollo. Pollo told me a long story about how the gang had decided to kill Angel at one point, a long time before. They had tied him in a chair already, Pollo said, and were planning to blow him away with a shotgun. Pollo was the one who talked them out of it. They listened to him finally because he, Pollo, was known to be a quiet kind of guy who never got in trouble. He made a deal to keep Angel out of trouble too. Many details of the story were lost in translation, and many were repeated for no obvious reason. The point that Angel was in the chair kept recurring. It seemed that being in the chair was very close to being dead.

Then Pollo asked me if I was a nervous person. He explained to me a test for nervousness. You take a plate and hold it between the fingertips of your two hands. If the plate moves, then you are nervous. Then the people I didn't know were gone and the Scotch was gone and I was not nervous. I began to shadowbox with Angel. He must have been drunker than I was because I was taking most of the points. That was an offense to his machismo. He got angry and began to crowd me toward a corner under the stairs. I was nervous again, but there wasn't much to be done short of blasting him. That would solve the immediate problem but probably be a losing gambit in the long run; you can't win at war, as they say. So I just kept hanging my left in his face and hoping for the best. When I ran out of room Angel took me down. I hadn't expected that and I bashed my head on the wall when I fell. Possibly I went out for something like a second. Then I could see Angel's face close to mine and I knew that he had forgotten where he was and thought he was really somewhere else, back in Germany perhaps, or in boot camp. Pollo stopped it and I was glad.

Then Angel went off somewhere and Pollo came upstairs with me. The knock had cleared my head to some extent and I began to give a lecture on the morals of fighting. Personal vanity, I explained, is one of the many things which are *not* worth fighting for. I remember repeating that idea over and over in several different ways, as if it were important that it be understood. I have a nervous habit of running my hands through my hair when I talk, and after a while I noticed that my fingers were coming away wet. I turned on a light and saw the blood on my hands, and I got rid of Pollo so I could try to figure out if I was hurt or not. It was an interesting dilemma. The most minor head wounds tend to bleed a lot, and I didn't think this one was serious, but then if you have a serious head wound, how good is your judgment going to be? I decided to go to bed and forget about it. In the morning my head had stopped bleeding and I didn't seem to be any dumber than I had been the night before. The only difference was that I had a blood-red ripple in my hair, as if I had dyed it that way.

After all this I took trouble to avoid Angel and Pollo. I can deal with the average social misunderstanding, but I don't like having my head cracked open. But Pollo would sometimes wait for me on the stairs above instead of the stairs below. He would listen for my key in the lock and dive in the door behind me. "You understand people," he said to me. I could have killed him. In too many ways it was simply not true. And even if I did understand people, what could I do about it? I didn't even know the language. I changed my pattern and I didn't see Pollo anymore until the night someone finally tried to break into my apartment.

I came home about ten that night and didn't notice anything wrong until I discovered my key wouldn't turn in the lock. I stepped back and saw that a triangle at the bottom of the door had been bent inward, fairly far. It was a heavy steel-sheathed door and it must have taken some force to do that, I thought. I had very little to lose but it still annoyed me that people were trying to break in, especially if I couldn't get in after them. The only way to get in now was to climb the fire escape outside and take down one of the gates from the windows. That was going to take some time, since you weren't supposed to be able to do it at all, but I didn't have any choice. I went to borrow a screwdriver from Benson.

Benson was home. He was cooking an octopus in a big pot on the stove. I told him the news and he picked up a coat and some long-handled pliers and came across to my apartment. In the entry he saw a car jack lying by the stairs and when he brought it up to my door we could both see what had happened. Someone had just tried to jack the door out of the frame. Benson clamped the pliers around the cylinder and strained at it. For a little man he had very big arms. The locking screws broke and the cylinder wound easily out of the lockplate and Benson reached in the hole and unlocked the door with his finger. It all took about a minute. I was glad it was something not everybody knew how to do.

We went inside and it was clear that no one had got in. Nothing was missing or even disturbed. Benson and I stood around talking about getting the door fixed, and how bad the crime was in the neighborhood, and how lousy the cops were, and what a shame it was that the price of octopi was going up so much. Then Pollo put his head in the door. He had picked up the car jack, and he told us it belonged to someone he knew, a black guy named Larry who lived at the end of the hall. I had seen him around. Pollo had been hanging out in a doorway and had seen someone, not from the area, trying to break into the cars parked on the street. Pollo had made sure they weren't the cars of people he knew and then had gone on down to buy some beer, so he hadn't really seen anything happen.

We were standing in the door talking to Pollo, and someone started up the stairs. When he got to the landing he looked at us and we looked at him and he turned around and left. We heard the street door bang shut and Pollo said, "That him."

Benson got a start on both of us and by the time I got out to the street he was already on the corner. He had taken off his coat to work on my door and he was standing there in a white T-shirt. It was cold and Benson looked small and lonely. I walked over to him and looked where he was staring. The other guy was halfway down the block. Something made him turn around, maybe he felt Benson's eyes on him.

"Why you looking at me," he screamed at us. "I do something?" Then he ran away.

I went into my apartment and thought things over. Then I cooked dinner and thought things over some more. I decided I wasn't in any big hurry to go to sleep behind a door I couldn't lock. I started to go outside and look at the street for a while. When I opened my door the door at the end of the hall opened too, and Pollo motioned for me to come inside.

Pollo was already too drunk to talk and it was easy to see why. There was a bottle of brandy on the table, and most of it was gone. Larry introduced himself and poured the rest of the bottle into a glass for me. I was in no condition to refuse it and besides it didn't seem likely to go much further. But it turned out that Larry also had a bottle of Canadian Club.

I drank some whiskey and looked around the room. There was some beat-up furniture, a huge white Bible on a stand, pictures of Larry's wife and children, the stereo I could sometimes hear through my wall, repeating the same two or three songs. We talked about the break-in a little bit. Larry had his jack back but he had lost a few small things from his car. But we agreed we had both been fairly lucky. Pollo got up to leave. He was having trouble keeping on his feet.

"Where you think you going?" Larry said.

"To my house to sleep," Pollo said.

"You going to wake up the people in your house."

"I just going in the door and getting in my bed."

"This house is your house."

So Pollo came back and passed out on the couch. Larry and I had another drink and he began telling me things. He had lived in the building for eleven years and when he moved in everybody was black. Now he was the last one. He grew up in Red Hook, an even worse place to live. Larry told me other things that had happened in the building: the time he had been held up with a gun in the entrance; the time his wife had sat behind the door and listened to someone pick one lock and luckily fail to pick the other. Larry had been in some fights and he showed me the scars of stab wounds on his hands. On his right hand there were only three fingers. Both hands were broken and clubbed. When we had finished a third of the bottle Larry began to talk about his wife, who was a Jehovah's Witness, and his children. He waved at the pictures of his family and explained to me how nothing could take them away from him. When we had finished two thirds of the bottle someone started to cough in the bedroom and I wanted to leave, but Larry wouldn't let me go before the bottle was all gone. It was dawn by the time he finally passed out and I walked around in the cold fog outside, hoping it might sober me up. I walked all the way to Greenpoint and had coffee and Danish at the Polish bakery, but it was no good. I went home and threw up for a while and slept for a couple of hours.

The break-in happened during Passover and because my landlord was Hasidic I couldn't get my door fixed for a week. You couldn't even talk to the man during the High

Holy Days. You couldn't even find him. I had to stay home
and stand guard over my typewriter. To kill time I took some
short walks through the Hasidic section of Williamsburg.
Time hadn't passed there since around 1800. On the last
day of Passover they all came out on the street in long black
coats and square hats trimmed with fur, the long beards and
the earlocks. You couldn't tell them apart from each other.
Some of them were arrested after the riot in Crown Heights,
but the plaintiffs couldn't identify them in the courtroom
and the case was finally dropped.

Pollo began coming around again during Passover. He made
a point of telling me that Angel had stopped drinking rum,
but I still didn't want to see Angel, and Pollo didn't bring
him by. He had decided that I was a serious person and now
when he came he talked to me about religion. He believed
firmly and literally in the doctrine of transubstantiation and
to prove the point he showed the scars of wounds he said
had been healed by the Host. He believed that his dead
father was in heaven and he hoped to see him there when
he died himself. I asked him why he didn't go to church and
he told me he worried that Jesus would think he was a
hypocrite for going to church after long nights of drinking. Which I could understand. Anyone could.

Then Passover was over and some Poles came and put in a
new door and Benson put in a new lock and I had a new key
and I got a new job, working as a janitor on Rivington
Street. The hours were different every day and my pattern
changed again and I didn't see Pollo again until the transit
strike, which began on April Fool's Day and lasted almost
two weeks. There were no trains and no buses running and
New York went completely crazy. During rush hours there
were cars backed up all the way to Philadelphia. People who
lived in the boroughs were walking to work over the bridges.

Pedestrian walkways that had been deserted for twenty years were jammed with people overnight. A few people died of heart failure when they got caught in the press on the walkways. Mayor Koch went down to the Brooklyn Bridge and spent an hour yelling at the crowd: "Don't give in. Don't give in." He didn't come to Williamsburg.

Every day I walked across the Williamsburg Bridge and down across Delancey Street and then two blocks up to Rivington. It took about an hour one way. On this bridge the walkway was never very crowded and the worst I usually had to worry about was being run down by a bicycle. One day two black guys tried to start a fight with me but it was downhill all the way to Delancey Street, and I made it. Because my work time was irregular I often had the whole bridge to myself. High above the East River, I could see the towers of Manhattan like figures from a dream. I could look back into Brooklyn and map the streets of my own area. Every other building in my neighborhood was a burned-out shell, but there were five Iglesias de Dios. The federal government had apportioned six million dollars to rebuild the area, but nothing had happened so far. I could look down on the disused train tracks and see the river moving beneath them. The tracks were still bright and shiny, because the MTA managers kept running a few trains over them to keep rust from accumulating. Below the tracks were the automobile lanes and I could always hear the cars droning steadily over the grating, an enormous hollow sound. I never saw a traffic jam on the Williamsburg Bridge. No one seemed to know it was there.

One night I came back very late, three o'clock maybe. There was no one on the street when I came down off the walkway. With no trains running over the el track it was eerily silent. I came to my building and peered in the little glass pane in the street door, to see if anyone was waiting inside. Since the time I talked to Larry I had been double careful. Larry himself was already dead by this time. He had been killed in a car wreck. I felt bad when I heard about it. But at least his wife had Jehovah and I thought that the Witnesses would take care of their own.

From my angle of vision the entrance seemed empty. I unlocked the door and gave it a little push to set it drifting. When I heard it touch the wall I knew that there was no one hiding behind it. I stepped into the doorway and looked over to the one corner that can't be seen at all from outside. Pollo was sitting there on the radiator, alone. He had on a gray military coat, which made him look formal. He didn't say anything. He nodded and waited for me to go up the stairs. I stood there and looked at him for what seemed like a long time. Finally I realized that this was the first time I had seen him completely sober.

"Why you sitting up so late?" I said.

"Just sitting here," he said. He jerked his head at the stairway. "I sit and listen. I hear the steps, and nobody."

I listened. It was deadly quiet in the building.

"I hear the wind in the street. I hear the cars going by. Going up and down."

We went outside and I sat down on the railing. Pollo walked around the corner and I lit a cigarette and looked up toward the sky. I could see the lights on the bridge arching away. The streetlight on our corner had burned out and that made the bridge lights seem brighter. There was a spring breeze, not quite either warm or cold, teasing the trash on the sidewalk. Pollo came back.

"Let me get one," he said. We sat and smoked, facing each other from opposite railings. On the other side of Broadway a pack of dogs passed under the streetlight and went into the shadows beside the diner there. There were at least five of them.

"A lot of dogs over there," I said, pointing.

"Yeah," Pollo said. "They call them the gang dog. They hang out all together like friends. They come out in the night and turn the cans over. They looking for food. They call them the gang dog."

The dogs came out from behind the diner and went away north on Berry Street. The wind picked up for a minute and then faded.

"There's a dog barking," Pollo said. "Barking around here all night long, don't let me sleep. You remember the dog I was keeping?"

I nodded. Pollo had kept a dog in the light well at the center of the building, back in December. One day the dog got out and nobody ever saw it again.

"I hear the dog barking and I wake up and think it him."

I looked down at my shoes, crooked through the railing.

"You know how they call the bridge?" Pollo said. It was his night for telling me what things were called, apparently. "They call it the forgotten bridge."

I looked up. There was a train coming down over the bridge and the sound of it filled the air above us. It was a long train and I could see lights on in every car.

"No people on that train," Pollo said. "Every night they running them all the way out to the end of the line."

"To keep the rust off the tracks," I said.

"Yeah," said Pollo. "Everybody saying the same thing. And you know why they saying it? Because it true."

"They call them the ghost train," I said.

"Yeah," Pollo said. "They go and they no pick up."

"They call them the ghost train," I said. That was true too.

The last time I saw Pollo was late in the summer. I came home just after dark and since it was a warm night I didn't go in right away. I stood by the pole of the broken street-light. I saw Pollo coming down the block. It being so warm he didn't have on a shirt. A couple of twelve-year-old girls were following him. They kept running up to him, giggling, and running away. Pollo came over to me and sat down with his back against the wall of the building.

"A nice night," I said.

"It warm," Pollo said. He looked cheerful. He was sober again. The girls shouted some things and ran away around the block.

"What's with them?" I said.

"Because I cut off my hair," Pollo said. He touched his head and smiled. His hair was cut very close, almost shaved.

"I don't care what they saying," Pollo said. "It too hot now for long hair."

We talked for a few minutes about Iran. Everyone Pollo knew was afraid there would be a war. Angel was still in the reserves. Pollo was nineteen and knew he was likely to get drafted in the first round.

"All I know is one thing," Pollo said. "If they going to make me go they better take some Jews too." He waved his hand toward where the Hasidim lived. "If they don't I going in there and kill some myself," he said.

I wasn't so worried about getting drafted. I was worried that maybe the world was going to get destroyed and I started talking about that.

"No," said Pollo. "He not going to destroy His world. He still like His world. He going to keep it a while longer."

"He'll destroy it when He comes again," I said. I wondered what Pollo would think of that.

"Maybe so," Pollo said. "I don't know. Don't even know when it going to be."

"Nobody does," I said. Pollo got up and came over to the pole. We were both looking up at the bridge. The double ribbon of lights arched away and blurred together; you couldn't see where they ended. The door banged and Benson came out on the street.

"Bensone know," said Pollo. He snickered. "Bensone know everything." It was the inverse square law again. Benson belonged to a different Iglesia de Dios.

"Eh, Bensone," Pollo shouted. "When God coming again?" Benson laughed at both of us.

I left Brooklyn.

I never saw any of them again, but I imagine they are all still there, except for Larry, who is dead. The bridge I know must still be there, since it is made of steel. One time I tried to count all the bolts that hold it together. Naturally I had to give up. At least I remember it now.

Zero db

❖

A GOOD SOUND MAN is someone who drives to work at twenty miles an hour.

Well, that's what they say. I am a sound man, though not necessarily and not always a good one. But I work. Correction. Until approximately seven o'clock this evening, I *did* work.

Twenty miles an hour. We may assume that that implies meticulousness, a close attention to detail, and great patience, near absolute.

Though some people say it merely means that a good sound man has his trunk full of expensive tape recorders.

Now I am sitting in a bar on 14th Street. I am here and come here often because of the bartender, who remembers what I drink (shot of bourbon and a beer chaser) and pours it for me without my having to ask. Ever. What you might call a high-fidelity memory.

Ordinarily I sit at the bar, where the service is faster. But tonight I am sitting in a booth in the back of the place. The seats in the booth are dark red vinyl, stained near black with smoke and spillage and age. Between them is a brown Formica table. There is very little light.

On the table is a shot glass and a beer glass, each half

empty. A couple of cigarette filters I have stood on end because there seems to be no ashtray for me to put them out in. And at the very edge of the table, a Nagra III tape recorder, my pride and joy.

The Nagra is sealed up in its black leather case. This is so no one will realize that I have several thousand dollars' worth of tape recorder here, because if they did, they might try to take it away from me. Now the tape recorder is running, and I am recording the sound of my own voice. I am using a lavalier microphone, about the size of a button on your shirt. Too small for anyone to notice, and besides, I have it cupped in my hand, practically inside my mouth. The lavalier is plugged into the line input on the side of the Nagra, and the headphones are plugged into the front. If anyone is watching, they may think I am listening to the radio.

Not so. The tape is running at 7.5 i.p.s., hi-fi not being a great issue here. Between one reel and the other the tape crosses three heads: record, sync (not now in use), and playback. Thus I hear my own words a half second after I say them. This situation can cause problems for novices, making it near impossible for them to talk, but I am accustomed to it.

I am whispering so softly that without the Nagra I could hardly hear myself. But with the Nagra, I can boost the signal. The needle on the VU meter is flicking just short of zero db, the point it must always approach but never reach. If the needle rises above that mark and stays there, the tape will be saturated. The tape will have received more information than it can absorb, and my words will degenerate into noise.

As it is, my whispering is loud and clear, what I imagine the wind might sound like if it could shape words.

I am hunched over the table, holding up the case flap with my thumb, peeping in at the front panel of the Nagra, where the VU meter and the level controls are. Above these instruments I can also see the three tape heads under clear plastic, with the tape running so reliably across them. The heads are, quite simply, beautiful. The face of each one resembles a little Mondrian painting. And the whole of the Nagra is beautiful as well. It is an apotheosis of form following function, the best tape recorder made. The Nagra will not fail.

Except, of course, in case of operator error.

It occurs to me that my greatest hope and ambition might be to emulate this beautiful machine. Or that I need no other reason for being other than to contemplate it. Though in fact, I do have another reason for being. Soon I will make a telephone call. But first I will finish this drink.

When I set my glasses back down on the table, it sounds like an explosion. Operator error. I will buy another. Always with one eye on the booth where the Nagra is waiting to see what more I have to say.

By any ordinary judgment, today has been a very bad day for me. Listen, and I will tell you what happened.

A week ago I finished a documentary shoot for Harold Brinks. Harold usually makes commercials. He is well suited to commercial shoots, where all the conditions are under his control and he can bully the cast and crew to his heart's content. But he is eminently unsuited to documentary work, where the conditions cannot be controlled and bullying is inappropriate. Especially a documentary shoot in a mental hospital.

I don't know why he decided to do it. Harold is a connoisseur of Good Things. Good Food, Good Wine, Good Music, Good Art selected by a Good Decorator on the walls of his Good Location in midtown. Maybe he thought it was time to go in for Good Works. I don't know and I don't care. I hate Harold, a stupid, venal man whose bad temper is his most valuable stock in trade. Harold is rather fat, balding, his skin taut and swollen like a pig's. His nose comes out in a big sweeping hook, then chops off at the end as though maybe it has suffered some sort of accident. Harold's nose makes him look like a tapir. I work for him because he pays. But there's a limit to everything.

This morning Harold calls me up and displays his bad temper and says that the sound from the shoot is a mess. Which I already know, because Harold had a cameraman who wouldn't take direction, so there was no direction, so I had to run tape hour after hour while the cameraman shot when he felt like it. Now Harold has discovered that there is a ten-to-one sound/picture ratio and no slates, and his intern can't sync up the rushes; in short, he wants me to come up and do it. Well, I would call that about a week of work, and I could use the money.

Sure enough, it is a mess when I get on Harold's flatbed. An hour of tape to five minutes of picture. Times fifteen. But I'm patient, meticulous, attentive to detail. I sit there watching picture for three hours, looking for a clue.

Then I find it. On the screen is a woman's face. Her mouth opens and closes; her throat throbs. Although I cannot hear it, I know that she is screaming.

It takes another hour to find the scream on all that tape. But when I find it, I enjoy it. The scream is pure, almost melodious. I am pleased to find that because I twiddled the knobs correctly when I taped it, it did not overload.

Now I know where to begin. After the scream there is a cut to a man talking. I watch his mouth until his lips shut firm.

The speech on the tape goes like this: "Listen. Listen. Listen. Anybody here that's got something to say . . ."

Anybody. Body. B. A letter where the mouth must close. I sync up, play back — it works. Not much, but it's a start.

By six-thirty I've synced up about twenty minutes' worth and put it on cores for coding. I pack up and get ready to leave. Harold comes boiling out of his office.

"Where you think you're going? Is it finished already?"

"Of course it's not finished," I say. "But I'm an hour into overtime."

"What overtime," Harold says. "This situation is your responsibility. It comes under your fee for the shoot."

"Oh no," I say, and I sit down. "Oh no, Harold, I don't know how to tell you this."

"Tell me what?" he says.

"Your nose, Harold," I say. "What happened to your nose? Did it get caught in a door somewhere?"

Harold begins to turn purple.

"Or did somebody maybe bite off the end of it one time? Could that have been what happened?"

Harold is beginning to sputter. I worry he may have a heart attack.

"You look a good deal like a tapir with that nose," I say. Harold is still inarticulate.

"A tapir is a South American pig," I explain. "It has a nose sort of like a little trunk. In case you didn't know. That's what I'm talking about. That's what your nose looks like, a tapir's nose."

That was the end of my employment with Harold, and probably with all of Harold's friends, who unfortunately are numerous and have given me a lot of work. That was an example of what Rosemary, to whom I will place a telephone call quite soon, would call self-destructive behavior.

Operator error, perhaps. I'll have another drink.

Getting back to the table, I see that two strange men have taken the booth behind mine. They are huddled so close together that I think they must be telling secrets. Very carefully, without turning around, I work the lavalier into the crack between the padding of my seat and the wall. There is noise in the headphones when I do this, like the microphone is being stamped on. But once I have it in place I can hear what the two men are saying.

"So why don't you use your Chink? The one that makes like Bruce Lee, I forget his name."

"Si Mung. Didn't you hear? He's no good anymore. Been out of the picture for four, five weeks."

"Didn't hear that. He get hurt?"

"He went mental. I thought you would have heard about it. Whole town must be laughing."

"No."

"Okay. Remember that guy Greg Tate? Lives out Flatbush Avenue. Biker. Kept a dog, a monster Doberman. Would kill you. Like a wolf, that dog."

"Haven't seen him around, recent."

"You probably won't. See, Greg had been owing us money. For months. Since even before we had Si Mung. He was hard to get to because of the goddamn dog. Which was attack trained. A dog a cop should have. Greg sits out on Flatbush Avenue, he laughs when we call up.

"Si Mung, he works for us a month, six weeks. Used him on people four or five times — we didn't hardly have to use him anymore. People knew. They would just pay up, no problem."

"That, I did hear."

"But, Si Mung . . . a very cold guy. I never much liked to watch him work. Like a machine ripping into somebody. It was weird."

"Self-control."

"Self-control like that, it makes me nervous. But he was sitting around, not much to do. So I talk to him about Greg Tate. Just, you know, see what he thought about it. And he goes into this heavy Chinese silence of his. Then gets up and says, Okay.

"Okay what, I say. I mean, what about the dog? How are you gonna handle it? I mean, I don't want the dog to eat you or something.

"Si Mung says, I don't wanna hurt the dog. That's all he

says. Goes out, stands next to the car and waits, like maybe he was a dog himself.

"So I think, Okay, I'm a gambler, right. I get in the car, drive Si Mung out Flatbush Avenue. Greg Tate is sitting right out there on the stoop. Got the dog on a leash, spiked collar on the dog. Greg got on a collar too, looks about the same. Si Mung gets out the car. Me, I stay in. Motor running too.

"Si Mung stands out on the sidewalk. Does his little Chinese breathing thing. Greg shakes the leash and the dog pulls out to the end of it and hangs there snapping at the air. More teeth than a shark, that dog.

"Si Mung looks up, says, I don't wanna hurt the dog.

"Greg laughs. Si Mung takes a step up the stairs. Dog comes off the leash, teeth everywhere, and Si Mung, I see this, puts his hands *into the dog's mouth*, like he's making his hands into a sandwich for the dog, and *rip*, the dog is running back up the steps. Howling. Si Mung broke his jaws, see. Had his hands cut up a little and that was all. Greg starts in the house after the dog, going for a piece we found inside later, and good thing he never got to it, a sawed-off shotgun. Si Mung caught him in the doorway. Kicked in a knee, broke his right arm, broke his left arm. Laid his head into the door-post and slammed the door on it till Greg Tate got no face left anymore. I mean, it was *flat*, where his face used to be."

"That's too much."

"Don't tell me. I get out the car, try to stop it, say, Si Mung, money's all we want, not dead people. But he didn't stop till, I don't know, he got tired or something. He turns around and says, I didn't wanna hurt the dog."

"Crazy. Like you said."

"Don't tell me. We got out of there clean, at least. Greg's in the hospital, never gonna pay anybody anything, maybe he's gonna die. But what the hell, it's an example for people. But Si Mung. He sits around the club a week, won't do anything, won't even say anything except, I didn't wanna hurt the dog. Si Mung, I say to him, you wanna eat, you wanna drink, you wanna shoot up, you wanna go out and beat somebody to death maybe? He says, I didn't wanna hurt the dog. Like that.

"Week of this, I say, Okay, let's go see about the goddamn dog. Back out Tate's place we find the dog lying down cellar, about half starved to death. Si Mung picks him up like he was a baby, carries him back to his place. Splints up the jaws, starts making the dog soup. And ever since that's the way it's been. Si Mung's good for nothing but making the dog soup. Even the *dog* is good for nothing anymore. All he can do is eat soup. It's a mess is what I'm saying. How should I know what to do?"

How should anybody? I pull the lavalier back through the crack and cup it to my mouth so I can hear myself whispering again. What a funny story. It is so funny that I am starting to cry. Big blubbering sobs come back to me through the headphones with a half-second delay. Doesn't sound good. It's overloading, and I reach out my thumb and turn the level down. I stop and listen and I forget to cry.

There are certain sounds that don't seem very loud at all, but somehow they can push the level up and up. Well past the machine's greatest tolerance, above and beyond all the headroom there is. These situations can be difficult to anticipate and control, and the possibility for operator error increases.

When I call Rosemary, which I will certainly do as soon as I stop sniffling, I will tell her that I absolutely cannot tolerate my life without her any longer. Nor should she be able to tolerate her own life without me. I will convince her that I still love her and that she must love me too.

We will not discuss the lawyer whom she plans to marry in the spring.

I may perhaps even promise certain things that I may not be able to deliver. To stop smoking, to stop drinking. To stop throwing away good jobs because of my bad temper. To make a serious and concerted effort to get into the union. To spend no more nights in this bar on 14th Street, whispering into the Nagra. To engage in self-destructive behavior no longer. So long as we both shall live.

At the phone booth, something new occurs to me. I take my telephone tapper from the side pocket of the Nagra's case and plug it into the line. I press the suction cup down over the earpiece of the phone and set the level to the dial tone. Now I will be able to record this important call. And listen to it at half-second delay.

I hear the coins fall, then the tones that represent the numbers. And now the phone is ringing. Three times.

"Hello," Rosemary says.

I listen. I can hear her breathe.

"Hello?"

I wait, expectant.

"Whoever you are," Rosemary says, "don't call again."

Dial tone.

Back in the booth it seems better to think about the dog with its broken jaws, to wonder if it will recover and hope by all means that it will. Water is lipping up to the lower rim of my eyelids and running down my face. I look around the bar, but no one notices; what I especially like about this place is that no one notices anything unless you hit someone. Through the headphones I can hear myself saying words like "Why will no one help me?" and "I've failed, I've failed." These words come back to me at half-second delay, fixed already on the tape and in the past, and they sound ugly and fatal. And the tape is overloading, distorting into noise.

Operator error. I turn the level down.

Over and over, I repeat new words:

I didn't want to hurt the dog.

I didn't want to hurt the dog.

And I feel much better. Twenty miles an hour. Perhaps I have only been going too fast.

I stop talking, turn the level up. The background sounds of the bar fill up the instrument: hiss of voices, clink of glasses, slow shuffling of feet. Room tone. On the lids of my closed eyes I see images.

I see the woman screaming in the film with all the force and power she can summon, without making the least sound.

I see the dog lying on the basement floor, breathing painfully, inaudibly, through his ruined jaws.

I see that Rosemary and I are walking arm in arm along a brick waterfront pier. The sun is low on the water, its reflections too painful to regard. Fat gulls swoop shrieking all around us. I see how the water meets the edge of the pier so precisely, no hint of drop or gap between them, the land dovetailed so smoothly into the sea.

I open my eyes, adjust the level. When I speak, the needle flicks toward zero and trembles exactly there, its perfect limit. I have just one thing more to say.

Listen. Listen. Listen. We can never be too attentive to our world.

III

Today Is a
Good Day to Die

❖

for Tom Brittingham

> *It looked bad for us. Then I heard voices crying in
> our language: "Take courage! This is a good day to
> die! Think of the children and the helpless at home!"
> So we all yelled "Hoka hey!" and charged on the
> cavalrymen and began shooting them off their horses,
> for they turned and ran. They were running toward
> their big party, and I could see many people were
> fighting over there, but everything was all mixed up,
> and you could not tell what was happening.*
>
> — Iron Hawk of the Hunkpapa Sioux,
> from *Black Elk Speaks*, edited by John G. Neihardt

"THE WEATHER CONTINUES POORLY," the lieutenant
writes. "Last night again it snowed, and this morning the
plains are trackless. The snow is as white and smooth as a
fresh starched sheet, though it does not resemble one. It resembles nothing, *tabula rasa*, a perfect blank. It is painful for
the naked eye to look at it for long —"

The lieutenant crumples the sheet of paper and sits for a
moment with it balled in his left hand. What he has done is
foolish, for paper is hard to come by here. However, it is cer-

tainly true that the words he has written are wrong, inappropriate for what is meant to be not quite a love letter to
the seventeen-year-old girl he likes to think of as his sweet-
heart, far to the east in Boston, a distance measured not only
in miles. He smoothes out the paper and folds it away into
a pocket; it is spoiled for this letter but he may yet find
some use for it. At any rate he can tear off the lower half
of the sheet. The lieutenant takes a fresh piece of paper
from his notebook and begins again.

"December 15, 1875." Ten days short of Christmas which
to be sure will be a cheerless holiday here. "If a certain someone only knew how much her image fills my thoughts" —
the lieutenant crosses out *thoughts* and replaces it with *eyes*,
but this is worse. He puts down the pen. It is difficult for
him to recapture the mood of a drawing room flirtation,
which now seems to depend more than anything else on the
narrow coziness of the house, the proximity of the bibelots.
The lieutenant rises and walks to the door of the low cabin
which serves as the junior officers' billet at Fort Robinson.
When he cracks the door his nose and lips are almost immediately numbed by the cold. From the door he can see
only the tracked and muddy ground of the yard, but
already this morning he has climbed the wall to inspect
what he has described in his first letter, the letter which
reflects his unease of mind so truly that he will never dare
send it to anyone. Though the sky is overcast, even here in
the yard the snow which has not been trampled shines
brightly enough to wound his eyes.

The lieutenant is just twenty-one years old, and he stands,
as one of his letters home might put it, on the threshold of
his life. He is a member of a minor branch of a reasonably
distinguished Massachusetts family, influential enough to
have procured him a commission at West Point, whence he
graduated without particular distinction in the spring of this

year. Now, with his academy record safely behind him, he is in a position to begin to do that family name some credit. But here at Fort Robinson he has learned to think of himself only in terms of his rank, that ideal expression of his uselessness.

And yet the lieutenant has come here almost entirely at his own request. He found himself bored to distraction by his first, eastern posting, though it was convenient both to his family and to that "certain someone," and though it might have been considered enviable by others in a similar position. He is not a reckless or adventurous young man, rather the reverse, but he craved more active duty, which in 1875 means either the equivalent of police work in the conquered South, or else a post on the western frontier, where Indian uprisings continue. The lieutenant puzzled his superiors by requesting a transfer to the Great Plains, colloquially known to many as the American Siberia, at the onset of what seemed likely to be a very harsh winter, and yet his request was granted. Now the lieutenant sometimes wonders dully what he has done to himself and why.

Almost daily the lieutenant rides out from the stockade, for the nominal purpose of exercising his horse, a reliable bay gelding with a white blaze in the center of his forehead. These excursions are somewhat irregular, but the post commander has little better use to make of the lieutenant, who is here on detached duty from the Seventh Cavalry, in the role of an observer. It is not a time when the commander wishes very much to be observed, and he is happy enough to be rid of the lieutenant for some part of each day.

Riding, the lieutenant keeps his distance from the Red Cloud agency, where the appearance of a solitary cavalryman might be provocative in these times, when Indian resentment of the gold miners swarming into the Black Hills is rapidly increasing. It does not occur to him that he will be more vulnerable if he encounters Indians on the open plain, and though he extends the distance and duration of his rides he happens to meet no one. The rides begin to last all day, and the lieutenant tells himself that he is hunting, though he is armed only with a saber and a Colt Peacemaker revolver (he is a poor pistol shot), and though he finds no game.

The lieutenant has come to Fort Robinson from Fort Abraham Lincoln, where most of the Seventh Cavalry is wintering. Winter camp did not suit him well. The enlisted men were an irregular lot, poorly disciplined, and he had difficulty controlling them. At Fort Lincoln the lieutenant reported to Major Marcus Reno in the absence of Custer, who was on a long leave in the East. He liked Reno well enough but found life on the weatherbound post stultifying, and when the opportunity came to go to Fort Robinson, where there was real activity, he jumped at it.

But almost all activity has ceased before his coming. The government commissioners have come and gone, their offer for the Black Hills rejected by the chiefs. Agent Saville reports that many Indians have left the reservation, probably to join the hostiles farther north, though weather has put a stop to that movement by the time the lieutenant arrives. By December, weather has put a stop to almost everything but waiting.

On Christmas Eve the lieutenant is drunk. A whiskey trader, one Willie Stubbins, has somehow made his way to the stockade for the occasion. Discipline is relaxed and Stubbins's trade is brisk. The lieutenant has outlasted most of the others, though not because he has a harder head than they. He does not. But he has refrained from drinking at all until very late in the evening when his lonesomeness finally drives him to it. Thus he finds himself sharing the keg with Stubbins before the fire in the long cabin where the other junior officers are already ponderously snoring.

Unaccustomed to the effects of alcohol, the lieutenant is so undone by Stubbins's cheap whiskey that he cannot concentrate on what Stubbins is saying. Stubbins seems to be claiming that he rode with Custer at the battle of the Washita seven years previously, where the Cheyenne chief Black Kettle was killed. Because he is too drunk to follow this tale, the lieutenant affects not to believe it, and Stubbins finally becomes offended.

"I'll prove it to ye," Stubbins says, and he removes something from an inside coat pocket to display before the firelight. The lieutenant shifts his head from side to side like a bird, trying to focus on the object: a brownish triangular sac with a black nub at the bottom of it.

"Feel of it," Stubbins says, and the lieutenant takes the thing in his numb fingers. It is wrinkled and leathery, the texture of chamois.

"Squaw titty," Stubbins says with some impatience. "Would make ye a nice tobacco pouch, say. How will ye trade?"

The lieutenant tries to fling the bag in Stubbins's face but misses by a yard. He stands up, sways, and catches himself against the chimney stones.

"Get out," he says. "Get out, get out." But Stubbins does not move from his stool. It is the lieutenant who has to leave, stumbling into the stockade yard to vomit, to kneel drily heaving for a long time over his own regurgitation, and finally to wash his face with snow.

Stubbins has fallen asleep across the hearth when the lieutenant comes back in, still very drunk but less violently so, with an odd floating feeling in his head. The whiskey trader sleeps on his back with his arms folded across his chest, almost like a corpse laid out for viewing, the lieutenant thinks, and he begins to stroke the handle of the revolver in his belt. Though he is a professional soldier, so to speak, Stubbins has taught him something new tonight: that it will indeed be possible for him to kill or maim another human being. Stubbins sits up suddenly and as if in accidental consequence of his motion his right hand draws a derringer from his left sleeve.

"Ye're drunk, boy, that's all," he says in rather a sympathetic tone. "It ain't as though they were Christians after all. Lay down a while and ye'll feel better in the morning."

On New Year's Eve the lieutenant abstains from celebration and so he is the first to rise on New Year's Day. Quietly he saddles his horse and lets himself out of the stockade. The snow on the ground is fetlock-deep and the day has a flickering brightness to it, from a cloud cover blowing rapidly over the sun. The lieutenant keeps his forage cap pulled low and squints against the occasional glare from the snow. The cold is severe but he has become inured to it during his long rides. Now he goes south at a walking pace, for just how long he does not know.

At length the horse stops, lowering his head, steam from his nostrils softening two hollows in the snow. The lieutenant turns to right and left, examining the pale featureless landscape all around him. He is sandwiched between a disk of snow and a disk of sky. The loud ticking of his watch distracts him and he draws it from his pocket. It is a handsome instrument; gold, a strutting peacock engraved upon its lid. Opening the watch, the lieutenant learns that it is a quarter to noon on the first day of 1876, though here on the vacant plain, he thinks, there is no date, no time.

Turning the watch in his hand, he looks at the miniature daguerreotype stuck to the inside of the lid, a full-length portrait of that "certain someone." The picture is too small and his eyes too blurred by cold for him to clearly discern her features; here she is only a wasp-waisted shape. Now for the first time the lieutenant sees not the queer Victorian furnishings of her dress but rather he imagines her body, the parts of it, its flesh and warm blood. He closes the watch and pockets it and then perversely recalls the look of the inhuman thing which Stubbins showed him. Horror at this association makes him whip his horse.

The lieutenant is galloping in no direction, only away from the thoughts which he hopes to leave in the emptiness behind him. The rush of air around his head makes his eyes water so that he is virtually blind. He is just beginning to wonder whether he or the horse is in control when he realizes that neither is because the horse has fallen and the lieutenant is rolling over and over in the snow. He is on his feet a second before the horse scrambles up and so is able to share in a flash of perfect empathy the dismay and disbelief which the horse feels when he puts his weight on the broken right foreleg and falls to the ground again. Now the lieutenant fires the best pistol shot of his career, drilling a dark hole in the white blaze, so that the horse jerks a time or two and then lies still. The lieutenant sobs a little, not from fear as well he might but from genuine remorse at the wanton waste he has made of his horse's life. Then he regains enough control of himself to reholster his gun.

The lieutenant understands that his position is poor. That last wild canter has obliterated his sense of direction, never strong, and he does not know the way back to the fort. It is close to noon, so he cannot reckon by the sun even if it were to shine. He starts to retrace his own wandering tracks, but before he has gone very far the rising wind begins to rub them out. The snow is deeper here, almost knee-deep. When the trail vanishes altogether the lieutenant stops. The ticking of his watch is loud and bothersome. He wraps his handkerchief around it, to muffle it a little, and plods on.

Because of the wind the lieutenant must walk with his head tucked into his overcoat lapel, and so he hardly sees anything. The snow dampens the hoofbeats so he does not hear them either and the first thing he is aware of is the voices shouting

"Hoka hey!" and other alien words that do not even register. He turns and the two mounted Indians are bearing down on him, the leader already leaning out to whack him on the shoulders with a bow. There is a painless tap and the lieutenant feels the flank of a horse brush by him. He faces forward again and sees the two riders wheeling almost in unison in front of him, stopping several degrees to the left of the straight line he is trying to imagine and walk. Both Indians seem young, no older than he. He looks up into their severe blank faces. Something is trembling beneath the surface of their perfect lack of expression but the lieutenant cannot tell what it is. He draws a deep breath and walks on.

The Indians fall in beside him, matching their horses' pace to his own. The lieutenant glances up at them occasionally, begins to resent how easily they are at home in this place, as he is not, though that is partly because they still have horses, he supposes. He keeps on walking; the Indians maintain their position relative to his. Now and again he hears them exchange a phrase or two in their own language, frequently followed by a laugh. The lieutenant suspects that he is being mocked. It has been some time since there has been any feeling in his feet. He can keep his hands alive by holding them inside his shirt, against his belly, but the numbness of his feet begins to worry him a little. The sound of his steps is almost entirely silenced by the snow, while the slow regular hoofbeats behind him are so faint that he might almost be imagining them.

Now one of the Indians is speaking louder, repeating a single remark, it would seem. The lieutenant cannot understand the words, but it gradually penetrates his mind that he is the one being addressed, just the same. However, he restrains himself from looking back. Up ahead, the horizon has grown no closer. The lieutenant stops, but a force of inertia drags him forward, so that he almost tumbles over, out of his tracks. He turns around to see that the Indians have pulled their horses up. Their faces are smooth, unlined, and, as he now realizes, somewhat younger than his own.

"I don't know," the lieutenant says, and all warmth drains out of him as if the plug of his being has been pulled and he sees the blanket of snow rising up to meet him halfway.

The lieutenant awakens to pain. An Indian is pounding his bare feet with his fists, but the pain comes from the stabbing of his reviving circulation. He sits up and pulls his feet away, but the Indian comes fluidly after him, still thumping. Recalling what he has heard of gangrene, the lieutenant submits, teeth clenched, and looks about for some distraction. They are sitting in a more or less dry patch behind a big rock, with a small fire burning beside them. A single horse is tethered nearby. The other Indian apparently has gone; there is no sign on the expanse of snow all around to indicate where he's vanished to.

When at last the Indian has stopped hammering his feet, the lieutenant swings around toward the fire and reaches for his socks and boots. The socks are dry, the boots warm now. The lieutenant draws up his knees and rests his chin on them. Across the fire the Indian sits cross-legged, absolutely still, but not stiff, by any means. After a time his hand glides easily forward to push a chunk of wood farther into the coals and then retreats into the limpid stillness of his body. It is ordinary, perfectly natural, this movement, but the lieutenant cannot stop himself from staring. He feels grotesquely awkward by comparison, even sitting still.

The Indian moves again, flicking a quick finger across the insignia on the lieutenant's sleeve, and says a word in an interrogative tone. The lieutenant nods reflexively, though he does not understand. The Indian hooks a thumb into the throat of his loose shirt and pulls out a necklace of teeth strung on rawhide, a few yellowed incisors from some meateating animal. Letting the necklace drop back into his collar, he smiles. The lieutenant shakes his head, bewildered. The Indian's smile collapses into blankness.

The lieutenant switches himself around and sets his back against the rock. In its lee, the wind has carved the snow into two ridges that meet at the apex of the triangle which encloses the dry area. The Indian emerges from his immobility again and moves away from the heat of the fire to smooth and pack a section of unmelted snow. When it is prepared to his satisfaction he pulls a quill from a braid on his sleeve and begins to make a design on the cleared surface.

The lieutenant moves around the fire, flinching a little from the pain in his feet, to see what he is drawing: a horseman with pistols and a saber and also a certain swagger in his attitude. The Indian completes the sketch with a series of long straight strokes coming from under the cavalryman's hat. He sits back on his heels and again touches the lieutenant's shoulder patch. It comes to the lieutenant that "Long Hair" is one of several Indian names for General Custer. He is nominally under this officer's command, though he has not yet met him.

"Custer," the lieutenant says, and the Indian flashes that same taut smile and nods. Leaning forward, he pats the sketch away with his palm and begins to work again. There are more images this time and they are more abstract, somewhere between articulated figures and either signs or glyphs. Cavalrymen, formed in a ring, hold muskets puffing smoke into a group of Indians they have encircled. Though the figures are not very detailed it is easy enough to make out the women and children. Outside the ring, to its right, the Indian sketches a bowed child's figure walking away, gestures from himself to this figure and back again.

The lieutenant pinches his lip between his teeth as he nods his comprehension, recalling Stubbins with a writhing of shame. Ahead of the child's figure the Indian now draws a dog, snarling, mouth full of many teeth. He repeats the child's figure, its head raised now, bow drawn. Then many figures surrounding the dog, and the dog's body filling up with arrows. Now with a sudden clarity the lieutenant recalls the story: how Custer's staghound Blucher was shot full of arrows after the battle of Washita and how deeply Custer grieved for the dog. More so than for the loss of Captain Elliot and his men on the same occasion, or so his detractors claim. The Indian makes a quarter turn away from the drawing and displays the necklace of teeth again, not smiling now.

"Yes," the lieutenant says aloud, nodding very deliberately. "So. You are the enemy." With no power to communicate their meaning, his words disappear as thoroughly as if they had not been spoken at all. The Indian lets the necklace drop and his eyes become inert, as if abruptly masked with some invisible lid. More words crop up in the lieutenant's head: *why, why me, why am I —, why would you —* He does not speak, and the words jounce against one another in his mind until all their expressiveness is worn away. The Indian's deep stillness resumes and holds until he turns back to the smoothed patch of snow and lets the flat of his hand fall on it at regular intervals from left to right, obliterating every trace of the drawing. Empty now and figureless, the snow grows luminous in the thickening twilight.

Giddy from the hardships of his day, the lieutenant must cling to the Indian's shoulders so as not to fall off his horse. He is unaccustomed to riding bareback and the movement of the naked animal beneath him is rather disconcerting. Darkness settles over them altogether as they ride in toward the fort. The lieutenant is alive with questions he cannot formulate. He may wish for the Indian's skill of communicating with sign and picture; however, what he wants to know he cannot even phrase in English. He remains a silent passenger until a faint glow appears on the horizon ahead.

When the Indian reins his horse to a stop the lieutenant

understands that he will go no farther and he slips down to the ground, landing with a painful jolt. He takes a few steps forward and then on an impulse about-faces and raises his right hand, palm out. The Indian and his horse have become a single shadow against the cloudy whiteness of the snow, and if there is any answering movement the lieutenant cannot discern it. He waits until the shadow has moved outside his vision, then turns and begins to go toward the lights of Fort Robinson, which he estimates is about three quarters of a mile away. His feet hurt him enormously, and he knows that means they are saved. The sky has cleared and the stars are almost painfully bright. The lieutenant feels that they are boring into him, and he hastens toward the fort on his agonized feet. Now he knows for certain that he is bound for survival, this time. Yet somehow he is rather surprised to find that the fort is actually coming nearer, instead of remaining always in the same position, as the horizon seems to do.

It is hot, a hot summer day, June 22, 1876. The lieutenant brushes mosquitoes out of his face as he goes toward the headquarters flag with the other officers. He walks with a slight limp now, having lost four toes from his left foot after his long walk of last winter. This council will be his first close sight of Custer, who has rejoined the regiment barely in time to relieve Major Reno of command for this expedition, and he is curious for a look at him.

The lieutenant has an image of Custer's long hair from pictures of his Civil War exploits which he used to look at as a boy, but today his hair is cut short. He wears a buckskin shirt and issue trousers and he has a habit of smacking his high boot tops with a quirt as he speaks. His manner of speech is a little orotund but the message is plain: there will be no further bugle signals, no straying, no unnecessary noise, lest the Indians become alerted of their advance and escape them. Custer has the attitude of a hunter toward prey, which inspires confidence in some of the men and increasingly vocal suspicion in others. He concludes his briefing by reading verbatim from a copy of *Army Regulations* a paragraph pertaining to extra-official grumbling among officers.

"It seems to me that you are lashing the shoulders of all to get some," says Major Benteen in a remarkably insolent tone. Benteen himself is a prominent grumbler. He believes Custer to be a glory hunter and therefore a dangerous man, and he is notoriously free with this opinion. Custer, surprisingly, does not call him out.

In the dusk the lieutenant walks alone to his tent. Since his return to the regiment he has not been sociable and in fact is beginning to make a reputation as a curmudgeon. He has given up even the effort to write letters home. The mosquitoes have thickened with nightfall and he moves his hand in a wavelike motion before his face to clear it. Farther upriver some of the younger officers have begun to sing, a raucous chorus. The lieutenant smiles when he passes Benteen's tent and hears the major snarling, "Why make the night hideous with song?"

From the start of this expedition the lieutenant has suffered from insomnia, though not because he is afraid. He is as brave as the next man, but he has allowed himself to do something no good soldier should: doubt the wisdom of the enterprise. His faith in manifest destiny is shaky, he feels little sympathy for the miners invading the Black Hills, and the Northern Pacific Railway, whose path this maneuver is partly meant to clear, now seems to him a long trajectory to nowhere.

Often he thinks of his encounter with the Indian in the snow, more often than he should, perhaps; indeed the memory is approaching the level of obsession. In fact, he would like to find the Indian again and pursue their conversation (if that is what it should be called), though he knows that his fellows would consider this wish insane. He pictures himself squatting on the ground before the Indian and figuring forth with a stick in the dust the images he cannot name. But no doubt the Indian has already gone north, along with most of the young men of the Red Cloud agency, to join the hostile tribes which the Seventh Cavalry is now seeking to engage. It is peculiar how the lieutenant almost misses him, how fervently he wants to devise some way of asking his advice. He has heard of the Indian practice of seeking guidance by going alone into the desert to dream. It is an idea which appeals to him, though for now he cannot even sleep.

On June 23 the column advances thirty-three miles along the Rosebud, not quite a forced march but a hard enough one. Custer is famous for driving men and horses, and for this the Indians call him Hard Backsides. The lieutenant, toughened by his winter rides, is less saddle sore than many.

The column passes three deserted villages during the day and the Ree scout Bloody Knife observes that the leaves on the wickiups' branches are nearly fresh. In camp that night there is anticipatory boasting among the men. The lieutenant makes a peremptory effort to silence his own unit and then, disgusted, walks away downriver. Some officers are easing their aches in the water, but the lieutenant, embarrassed by his toeless foot, will not join them. He limps around a bend of the Rosebud, out of earshot of the camp. The melted snows have fed the grass and the land is lush and fecund, yet for the lieutenant this remains a barren place, as if winter has left him with some permanent form of snow blindness.

After a twenty-eight-mile march on June 24 hardly anyone is pleased when Custer breaks camp after dark for a stealthy advance westward toward the Little Bighorn. The regiment moves out to the tune of suppressed swearing. Because of heavy cloud cover it is dark as the inside of a pig's stomach, so the lieutenant hears someone near him remark. The column moves as a single serpentine organism led by the Ree scouts at its head. It is two A.M., the lieutenant discovers from his watch, when they halt at the first rise of a slope. Someone up the line hisses to him to put out his light.

Again he is unable to sleep and dawn comes to him as a relief from the effort. Custer rides from troop to troop, advising the officers that the scouts believe the Indians to be only a few miles ahead. The lieutenant saddles up and moves with the line to the crest of the ridge, from which he can look out over the low rolling hills to the mountains beyond. Possibly because of his fatigue the edges of his vision seem to sparkle and hum. A little dizzy, he lowers his head and keeps his eyes fixed on the sego lilies entwined in the rich grass, as the column moves down the draw toward the Little Bighorn. Soon he is so much at ease that he half dozes in the saddle. When Custer divides the regiment into battalions he obeys with the unconsciousness of a sleepwalker.

Reno's troops have crossed the river. The lieutenant is startled out of his daze when word comes down the line that Bloody Knife and the Rees have spotted a big village just ahead. He himself can see the tops of the tepees when the order to charge is sounded. Spurring his horse forward, he draws his saber and holds it stiffly erect before him like a flagpole, as if he has no idea what to do with it, which is the case. Today is his first engagement with any enemy. The cavalry sweeps into the village, knocking over tepees and scattering Indians who, utterly surprised, are trying to arm themselves and catch their horses. There is a staccato noise of Springfields firing all around.

The lieutenant's saber strikes something which he has not seen and is torn from his hand with a painful wrench to his wrist. Mounted Indians are attacking out of the dust to his left, and with futile West Point precision he identifies the maneuver as a flank attack. A big Indian leader is riding toward him, swinging a hatchet, sinking it into this or that cavalryman. The lieutenant breaks the fascination that for a moment holds him fixed to the spot and turns his horse to flee.

He pulls his horse up just behind Reno, in a sheltering grove of pines. Reno is shouting, trying to re-form his troops. The lieutenant leans over the shoulder of Bloody Knife, straining to decipher the orders, and sees the scout shot full in the head, splattering Reno's face with blood. Now the Indians are among them again, and the cavalry is in full flight for the river. There are already uniformed bodies staining the water when the lieutenant gallops by with others toward the bluff. He feels a curious sense of déjà vu when his horse disappears from under him and he is flung forward up the rocky slope. An arrow vibrates in the ground next to his knee, and the lieutenant picks himself up again and scrambles for the hilltop.

The bluff is defensible enough, though far from perfectly secure. The lieutenant helps supervise the quick raising of barricades made from hardtack cases and dead horses and anything else at hand. Reno seems confused, perhaps demoralized, and when Benteen's battalion reaches them in the late afternoon it is Benteen who takes over effective command, ordering the digging of ditches and further bolstering of the barricades. They are unlikely to be overrun in this position but the hill is altogether surrounded now and painfully exposed. The soldiers are so exhausted that many drop asleep in the midst of their digging despite the bullets and arrows that continue to whir among them until it is completely dark.

Among those who remain awake that night there is a low and constant litany of complaint, for many are convinced that Custer has abandoned them. Ugly stories of the commander's past lapses are revived, rehearsed, and adorned. Weary of this tune, the lieutenant seeks out Major Benteen and volunteers for a sentry post. Under cover of the dark he hoists himself onto the shoulders of a dead mule to look down the bluff toward the river. The Indian camp is bright with firelight and there is celebratory dancing. The lieutenant watches, almost wistfully, until a noise immediately before him makes him draw his Colt.

"Halt," the lieutenant whispers, and out of the dark come the words "Don't shoot." It is Michael Boylan, a trooper from the lieutenant's unit, who has spent the afternoon hiding in the brush on the slope along with a few other stragglers from Reno's battalion. Boylan is parched with thirst, but the lieutenant must tell him that what water is left here is reserved for the wounded. He sends Boylan deeper into the lines to sleep, staying on the barricade himself. Toward dawn Benteen sends him a relief, but he remains wakeful, watching the Indian fires burn down to coals.

Many horses are shot and killed when the attack resumes at first light; they stand too tall for the barricades and cannot be protected. The surviving horses are uncontrollable and their panic spreads to the men. The lieutenant moves from group to group, trying to maintain morale and order, crawling on his hands and knees, as everyone who wishes to move must do. What bothers him more than anything else is his dry and swollen tongue.

Cover on the slopes is favorable to the Indians, and snipers have come near enough to pick off troopers inside the camp.

The lieutenant joins a group led by Benteen for brief sorties against them. Among the other volunteers he vaults the barricade and runs stooping into the bushes, discharging his revolver at random, for he cannot see a vestige of the enemy. After each of the three charges he feels some vague sense of frustrated expectancy and later he will realize that he has been waiting for a bullet or arrow to strike him.

At noon the attack ceases, abruptly and for no apparent reason. The lieutenant takes a risk and for the first time in many hours straightens his back to stand fully erect. Along the riverbed the Indians are striking their tents and loading travois, and the lieutenant is awed by their number: thousands of people and thousands of horses are coalescing into a laval flow toward the Bighorn Mountains.

Even when the plain below has emptied, Reno orders the position held. In the afternoon he dispatches a few men to the river for water, and they return unmolested, bringing great relief. Nevertheless the remnants of the battalion spend another night on the bluff, and it is not until the next morning that outriders from Gibbon's column come to relieve them and bring news of the massacre of the rest of the Seventh Cavalry.

Along with the other officers of Reno's command, the lieutenant rides back with Gibbon's scouts to help identify the bodies. It is a silent expedition, hushed by disbelief at first and then by creeping dread. The lieutenant, virtually sleepless for four or five days now, is merely numb.

The first bodies lie in a line along a shallow declivity which runs from the riverbank up to the peak of a low hill. Most of the two hundred and fifty corpses are scattered near the top. They have all been stripped to the skin and scarcely a scrap of leather or cloth remains to them. All that is left is paper money, blowing fitfully over the dead like leaves. There have been extraordinary mutilations, furthered by the picking of the birds, but it is not that which impresses the lieutenant. What strikes him most vividly is the piebald coloration of the corpses: the hands and faces deeply tanned and the rest of the wretched forked bodies an unseemly white, like something that can only thrive in darkness.

The other officers have dismounted to begin the dreary work of identification, but the lieutenant stays in the saddle and rides a little away from them. At a short distance he stops and turns back to look again. The scene is unreal, dreamlike, yet if it were a dream, he thinks, it would require a vision to explain it. The lieutenant touches his body here and there and finds that he is still substantial, though he is quite certain now that his life is no longer his own. He rides around the crown of the hill, out of sight of the others, and urges his horse to a canter. No one has missed him, and a few hours later when heads are counted he will be numbered without much question among the majority, the dead.

Toward evening the lieutenant comprehends his first mistake and gets down from his horse. He turns the animal to face the east and slaps him on the rump. However, the horse follows him toward the distant mountains, nuzzling at his neck. The lieutenant whirls and slaps him across the nose but the horse is only momentarily discouraged and keeps following. Finally he must fire a shot between the horse's ears to stampede him back in the direction of the regiment. When the horse has vanished into the middle distance, the lieutenant faces smartly about and marches forward, favoring his bad left foot somewhat. Alone on the plain that night he sleeps a little, but if he dreams he remembers nothing of it.

In the morning it is very hot and the lieutenant sweats inside his uniform when he begins to walk again. After an hour he has another notion and he empties out his pockets, flinging away his pistol, knife, a pen, his currency and coins, that scrap of paper which describes the winter snow, reserving only his watch.

He limps along the trail of the Indian hordes, in the

middle of the swath they've cut across the plain. Their horses have eaten the grass back to the roots, so that the land is now almost as bare as the lieutenant feels it ought to be. And yet he knows now that this land is alive with spirits! It is not that there is nothing here but that he has failed to see it. Or perhaps the Indians have taken the gods of this place with them; certainly they have left little else behind.

It is noon by his watch when the lieutenant stops to remove his clothing: the uniform tunic, the undershirt, and the boots and trousers. He fastens the chain of his watch around his neck to wear it as a pendant. Dressed only in his linen, he proceeds. The mountains seem to have come no nearer these two days, but still he marches on. At first the sun is grateful to his skin; not before midafternoon does it begin to scorch and burn.

He has had no food, no water. There is sure to be some stream nearby but he has neither the wit nor the will to seek it. Toward evening he kneels and finds a pebble and places it in his mouth. A little flow of liquid starts up around the stone. The lieutenant looks up from his crouch, squinting against the setting sun, and sees the first vulture hanging immobile like a blot on the cloudless blue sky.

By the third day he begins to stagger and can no longer walk very far at a stretch. He will begin to reel to the left, sinking over his bad foot, and will have to either stop and rest or fall. Great watery blisters have risen on his face and chest and back, some already broken and beginning to bleed. The watch around his neck weighs like a millstone. At intervals he thrusts out his tongue and glances at the tip to confirm that it is turning black. The vultures gliding above him have increased in number.

When the lieutenant falls and cannot get up again he finally understands the last thing that is wrong. It is the ticking of his watch, that unbearably regular sound which must soon madden him. He crawls to a nearby stone and pounds the watch against it until the ticking stops. Exhausted, but quite pleased, he rolls over onto his back, and in the blessed silence his vision comes to him. He sees a wraithlike shape, not soul but a dark devouring shadow, rise out of his suppurating body and march inexorably over the mountains to the sea. The lieutenant is happy that this thing has left him, and relieved that its future will never be his own. He is glad that he will never reach the mountains now. He is even grateful when the first buzzard lands beside his outstretched arm with an ungainly flop. *Brother, I greet you,* the lieutenant says, hearing the words plainly, though his tongue has swollen past the point of actual speech. *Take and eat what God hath given thee.*

JOHN·DAVID·MORLEY

THE·CASE·OF·THOMAS·N

'DISTINCTLY COMPELLING' *Observer*

Thomas N took his seat at nine o'clock on Monday morning knowing no better than anyone else in court if he had committed the crime for which he was being put on trial.

He appeared to have come from nowhere, to have no friends, no name, no sense of his own identity. There was no personal pronoun in his universe. His doctor suggested that he didn't know who he was because he feared 'anything that objectively demonstrates his existence'.

So when he wakes up one morning next to a dead girl, he naturally attempts to cover up all trace of his presence. But he finds himself in the dock for murder, in a court where identity itself is on trial: Thomas's, the murderer's, and that of the enigmatic figure in the shadows.

'A clever, ambitious novel from an excellent writer whose previous work of fiction, *In the Labyrinth*, established his vision of a Kafkaesque world of uncertainty' *The Times*

0 349 10051 9   FICTION   £3.99

SAINT HIROSHIMA

LEIGH KENNEDY

As a boy, Phil failed to summon up enthusiasm for baseball. He preferred Chopin. He was nurturing a musical conspiracy with the universe. Katie felt she was the victim of another sort of conspiracy. Her childhood imagination had forever fused together everyday accidents with the billowing mushroom of Hiroshima. The threat of nuclear holocaust stalked her at every moment. Meanwhile Katie stalked Phil.

By the time Phil was ready to go East and make the world proud of him, no ordinary bond had grown up between Katie and himself. They understood each other's obsessions. Phil's keyboard was Katie's bomb shelter and, together and apart, from the Cuban missile crisis to the raid on Tripoli, the curious duet played on . . .

0 349 10064 0   FICTION   £3.99

Also available in ABACUS paperback:

FICTION

ST HIROSHIMA	Leigh Kennedy	£3.99 ☐
AN IRRELEVANT WOMAN	Mary Hocking	£3.99 ☐
AWAY FROM HOME	Penelope Farmer	£3.99 ☐
A YEAR OF SILENCE	Madison Smartt Bell	£3.99 ☐
A DARKNESS IN THE EYE	M. S. Power	£4.50 ☐
PEOPLE FOR LUNCH	Georgina Hammicks	£3.99 ☐

NON-FICTION

WHITE BOY RUNNING	Christopher Hope	£3.99 ☐
EASY MONEY	David Spanier	£3.99 ☐
ZOO STATION	Ian Walker	£3.99 ☐
THE PANAMA HAT TRAIL	Tom Miller	£3.99 ☐
UNDER A SICKLE MOON	Peregrine Hodson	£3.99 ☐
AN UNFINISHED JOURNEY	Shiva Naipaul	£3.50 ☐

All Abacus books are available at your local bookshop or news-agent, or can be ordered direct from the publisher. Just tick the titles you want and fill in the form below.

Name _____

Address _____

_____

Write to Abacus Books, Cash Sales Department, P.O. Box 11, Falmouth, Cornwall TR10 9EN

Please enclose a cheque or postal order to the value of the cover price plus:

UK: 60p for the first book, 25p for the second book and 15p for each additional book ordered to a maximum charge of £1.90.

OVERSEAS & EIRE: £1.25 for the first book, 75p for the second book and 28p for each subsequent title ordered.

BFPO: 60p for the first book, 25p for the second book plus 15p per copy for the next 7 books, thereafter 9p per book.

Abacus Books reserve the right to show new retail prices on covers which may differ from those previously advertised in the text or elsewhere, and to increase postal rates in accordance with the P.O.